Jon Grainge's

Echoes

from a

Silent Enemy

"Echoes from a Silent Enemy"

Published by blurb.com
Front cover: Ariel view of GCHQ, Cheltenham, Airbus A380 and laptop

The
"European Photo-Book"
collection

Jon Grainge's

Echoes

from a

Silent Enemy

Echoes from a Silent Enemy

This book is a work of **pure fiction** and is the result of the author's rather vivid imagination. All of the characters are fictitious and are a product of the author's imagination or are used fictitious. Any resemblance to actual people is entirely coincidental.

This is a book of Fiction

The
"European Photo-Book"
collection

Further action-adventure novels available in this collection

Appointment in CAIRO
"Revolution is in the Air"
Appointment in DOUZ
"Death of a Colonel"
Appointment in PUERTO BANUS
"Double Abduction"
Appointment with the FAITH
"An Eye for an Eye"
A Voice from Heaven
"Confusion over Iran"
Counter-Strike
"The World holds it's Breath"
Fateful Decision
"Exposed from within a Buried Secret"

The "European Photo-Book" collection

Selection of **E-Books** for
download onto your ipad

www.blurb.com/user/store/hightrainman

To read full details of these and other adventure e-books for sale
please go to the website.
(All cards taken)

Aviation .. Marine .. Travel .. HST .. Cocktails .. Fashion Models

The" **European Photo-Book**" collection

Preface

GCHQ intercepts a series of messages, known in the trade as **Echoes**, from the world's most wanted terrorist, Abasin Zadran based in the middle-east and following intensive investigation fall upon a cyberplan to bring down two airliners, including the new British Airways A380, at London's Heathrow Airport.

In their resolve to capture Zadran, MI6 stumble upon a further plan for the Egyptian Brotherhood to invade Israel with British warplanes.

Will either of these plans come to fruition?

After reading this book continue onto

"Appointment in CAIRO"
(Revolution is in the Air)

The **"European Photo-Book"** collection

Contents

The **"European Photo-Book"** collection

List of Main Characters:

Jim Norris ......Senior Operative at GCHQ
Florence D'Arcy .. Middle East Section Manager GCHQ
Dean ...... Operative at GCHQ
Abasin Zadran ...... Leader of Al-Mawla
Mrs Jessica Billgate-Hardman .... Head of MI6 ('B')
Damian Arbuthnot ...... MI6 agent (Cairo)
Fiona Campbell ...... The Home Secretary
Denis Morrison ...... The Prime Minister
Alistar Bennett ......Defence Secretary
Kevin McCloud ...... Senior Controller of MI5
Sir Philip Newman ...... Director General of GCHQ
Lesley Billington ......Police Commissioner
Mohammed X ...... Leader of Egyptian Brotherhood
Asphan Rachid ...... Egyptian software specialist
Group Captain Barton ...... Member of M.A.R.S.
Flight Lieutenant 'Ace' Wright ...... Chinook pilot

Chapter One

A Lead

Location: Cheltenham

It was a dull and depressing day with the cold September rain beating down hard on the windscreen of his 2004 BMW 318SE as Jim Norris left the comfort of his luxury and immaculately presented two bedroomed apartment in Pittville Circus Road and jumped into the beige leather drivers seat. The short two and a half mile journey to work would normally take him fifteen to twenty minutes but in the inclement weather he had allowed a few minutes more. The time was 0830 and on this Friday 13th Jim found the traffic unusually high. Once through the traffic lights outside Cheltenham Boy's School the traffic cleared somewhat until he hit the main A40 leading toward Gloucester ..then it became a crawl allowing Jim plenty of time to reflect a little upon his career thus far with GCHQ.
It had been four years since he graduated from Bristol University having attained an Hons. Degree in languages, in particular Spanish and Classical Arabic. With no particular career path in mind when applying for entrance to the Uni, he just had this interest and hankering to speak more than just English. The young Mr Norris was a perfectionist and his attention to detail in everything he did was legendary within the family circle, to the extent that Natalia, his current live-in girlfriend whom he came across whilst out drinking in a local club in Cheltenham, had begun to question her relationship. She was almost the total opposite to Jim in her domestic habits giving rise to more than the usual upsets expected in the normal household.
Once he left the family nest in Four Oaks, being a suburb of Birmingham, Jim headed straight to the

campus at Bristol and began his studies. Neither his father, a civil engineer or mother who had been a check-in girl at Birmingham Airport, had imposed the slightest career pressure upon their only child. All Jim knew was that he had a leaning toward international communications and felt that Spanish, in particular, and Arabic could be beneficial in carving out a direction with which he could earn a living.
The three year course changed the boy into a man and being a quick leaner found it relatively easy to attain a double Hons in both languages.
Whilst on campus and nearing his final exams Jim had been causciously approached by a smart, middle-aged, gentleman, calling himself Mr Smith, with the intent of persuading Jim into a career in the civil service and to be based at one of the UK's top establishments in nearby Cheltenham. Being from a sheltered 'Brummy' background the young Mr Norris had not the faintest idea of what went on at GCHQ but having been advised of the opportunities open to him through his language skills, Jim eventually agreed to embark upon a year's trial once his BA's had been confirmed.
That was four years ago and in that time he had risen to the exalted position of Senior Operative, however the mundane activity of covert listening, listening and more listening to international conversations and
e-mails was beginning to be unfulfilling to the evermore expecting Mr Norris.
The traffic began to slowly edge it's way forward. The mixture of the dark morning and pouring rain together with the familiar density of traffic was playing upon Jim's concentration to the extent that the car behind had to toot his horn to awaken him from his

day dreaming.
It was now 0855 as displayed by his Seiko chronograph which started to unnerve the usually calm Mr Norris. For the first time in his working life he was going to be late for his clocking-on and this was not going to look good on his record. GCHQ were very strict about punctuality, but what could he do to avoid the traffic, nothing. A little sweat began to appear on his forehead.
Eventually the BMW was able to turn into the short drive that led to the security gate where the familiar burly, uniformed Sergeant Bush sat at the kiosk window,
"Good morning Mr Norris. May I see your ID again please."
" Not such a good morning in this rain Brian," Jim replied.
"Can't win them all , Sir. Carry on and have a good day" Bush wished the evermore anxious Norris and slid the glass inspection window closed.
Once the 318SE was neatly placed in it's designated space in the senior staff car park, the now slightly frought Mr Norris quickly grabbed his raincoat, slammed the car door closed, pressed the auto doorlock on the keyring, listened for the bleep, bleep and ran to the main entrance of the modern and impressive circular building (nicknamed the doughnut) with his coat slovenly drapped over his shoulders.
"Good morning Mr Norris, Sir" spoke the smartly dressed security officer.
"Not so good, I'm bloody late today for the first time" replied Jim.

"Don't worry sir I don't think you are the only one" the officer reassuringly advised Norris.
Once Norris had placed his ID card and left palm on the glass top of the scanner and allowed the red laser beam to correctly identify the code secretly planted within the card and compare various lines implanted at birth on Norris's index and forth fingers , he was permitted to enter the atrium of the huge glass fronted building. Immediately he ran down the stairs to GL1 level and along the rather stark and clinical corridor to the office marked 'Middle-East' where he slid his ID card into the wall mounted clock-in computer. The digital readout came up 0912. Twelve minutes late!
The interior of 'Middle-East' section, being the largest and currently most important scene of operations, was vast incorporating around twenty two operatives , all of a lingual eliteness, with each having their separate circular glass cubicle of pure serenity allowing prolonged periods of concentration. Jim had the priviledge of his own relatively plush compact but nevertheless comfortable cubicle. However before going to take up his usual position at his console he best thought to call in to advise his boss of his late arrival in order to placate his, up to now perfect, attendance record as best he could.
Popping his head around the door he immediately glanced at the beautiful blonde, with whom he had delusions of grandeur at possibly asking out on a date, sitting at her desk,
"Good morning Florence. I really must apologise for my late arrival this morning but the traffic was just terrible."
Removing her glasses and casting her gaze at the door,

"Hi, Jim. Oh don't worry most of us had the same problem due to a terrible accident on the M5 causing a tailback onto the A40. By the way are you still coming to the office party next week?"
With a sudden sense of elation welling inside with interest the beautiful Florence was apparantly showing in him,
"Yes of course, Florence. Hopefully I will have a dance with you."
"Of course Jim. By the way call me Florie. You had better start work!"
Settling into the leather office chair Jim switched on his receiver equipment and placed the headset neatly on his head. The previous few weeks of international data traffic that he manged to pick up was of a mundane magnitude and of no particular interest. A few conversations between some Libyan officials, the odd lurid e-mails between known villains and some advisories from the Lebanese theatre .. standard traffic and of no threat to the UK. Jim assummed that this level of data importance would continue on this friday ... he was wrong!

It was the **13th**!

The morning shift passed without any undue events. There was plenty of traffic and interceptions but nothing that contained any 'magic' words that would initiate the computer to advise a more closer manual observation. For the majority of the time that morning all Jim could do was to think about what the lovely Florie had asked. Was she interested in him or was it just a polite time filler or did she want the section to have a good representation at the party.

For the past year since the Miss D'Arcy had been upgraded to the exalted position of Section Manager from her previous position of Senior Analyist of the Central European section, the normally quiescent Mr Norris had been having some rather perverted intentions towards the half French beauty from Paris. Despite the fact she was nearly ten years older than himself and had been through a messy divorce he fancied the knickers off her; so did most of the male staff in 'Middle-East' section but they were all married and illicit affairs were not sanctioned in this high security environment.

It was during one of these day dreaming moments of ecstacy whilst late into the afternoon shift, that Jim suddenly had his attention interrupted with the intermittent bleep from his Honeywell **z** series computer system. Immediately, but without undue speed, Jim homed in on the highlighted 'magic' word that had been recognised. "هدف" which translated to the word "Target".

With his usual responce to this situation Mr.Norris isolated the Farci (Iranian) conversation in question and listened intently to it's contents endeavouring to establish the source and destination of the transmission. An automatic pre-programmed function of the Honeywell was to record any transmissions containing these suspect words.

The general gist of the message content was not in itself that interesting, however from Jim's experience in analysing verbal conversations it appeared to him that this particular conversation was deliberately spoken in code which warrantied closer attention as this was a touch out of the ordinary.

The duration of the complete conversation was less than one minute but as soon as the transmission died Jim isolated it to a separate computer for a series of replays hoping that he might gain further information. He did not. He then instructed the Honeywell to establish the source of the transmission and possibly the recipient if enough conversation had taken place. The frequency of 113.786 mhz was confirmed which did not show upon any previous record. They had tracked a new operator.

Eventually the source was established ... it was from an unknown area north-west of Tehran and from the dialect of the recipient Jim judged it to be a Cairo based form of Classical Egyptian Arabic.

Putting all the evidence together presented Jim with a scenario that would be worth reporting to Florence. It would also give him an excuse to spend some time with her.

It took all of around an hour for Florence, having considered the evidence and coupled the locations with the fact that a fresh uprising in Egypt was considered imminent , was finally persuaded to issue a semi-threat status to this tracking which would entail several other operatives concentrating their endeavours on these areas. This further meant contacting the NSA (National Security Authority) in Washington, USA to request they re-direct their satellite network to concentrate on the Iranian and Egyptian theatres. It would be their interceptions that would be relayed directly to GCHQ and then copied to Washington, such was the inter-oceanic cooperation between two of the cyber-space superpowers.

The day ended peacefully with both Jim and Florie

looking forward to their week-end whilst leaving the business of awaiting another message to those on the Saturday and Sunday shifts.
Miss D'Arcy, who incidently also lived in a select area of Cheltenham, Montpellier, treasured her days away from the stress of the 'doughnut' with this particular week-end being no different. Saturday afternoon, as the weather had improved for a couple of hours, was the time she decided to pop into several of the designer shops in Promenade (main shopping street in Cheltenham) in order to find a new outfit for the forthcoming office party which was to be held on the evening of September 21st in order to celebrate the seventieth anniversary of the naming of the organisation as GCHQ. The beautiful Miss D'Arcy, an intelligent student from the Sorbonne who had worked her way up through the French military and intelligence service in Tunis to her present position of Section Manager, elected to choose a conservative knee length black dress by Karen Miller. This was her way of playing 'safe' amongst all the plethora of overly active, but married, men within her section.
At the other end of the scale poor old Jim could not remove the desirous thoughts from his head and spent much of his week-end considering the in's and out's of a plan of attack to entrap his prey at the forthcoming office party. He finally elected that his best approach would be to encourage a little Russian vodka to loosen the slightly cold exterior of the normally icy Miss D'Arcy and to then enlist his gentlemanly talents into seducing a kiss from her and then take it from there!
Monday morning came round only too soon and true to the British weather after a week-end of rain the sun

decided to shine on the commencement of the working week.
The day , as did the next two, turned out to be normal without any out of the ordinary or undue alerts. Florie was beginning to have second thoughts about her actions of contacting the NSA the previous friday but was prepared to stand-by her decision till the end of the week, afterall this patient work was the purpose of the intelligence service., she thought to herself trying to convince her more questioning half that she was doing the right thing.
By thursday mid-morning the same routine messages intercepted from Damascus, Lebanon and Iraq continued with little content of interest which only added to the slight atmosphere of unease now creeping into the section as a whole , until the Honeywell at cubicle 1 addressed the attention of the ever observant Mr Norris with it's bleep.
Another magic moment, but this time a phrase, was highlighted, "لنـــدن الهـــدف" (London target). The recording of the conversation by the **z** series was confirmed as Jim diverted his full attention to listening in and interpreting the arabic message. Once again Jim was convinced it was in code. It was more lengthy than the previous interception but the content and style of coding led Jim to believe the it was the same two people that had conversed before. The conversation was being carried out on mobile phones , which would be easy for GCHQ to later trace should they be from a contracted network.
Once the call had been completed Jim immediately ran to Florence's office advising her to listen to the recording. This she did and was interested as it further

vindicated her earlier decisionto inform the NSA.
With the full interpretation laid before them both on her desk it read,

Message 1213hrs 113.786hz
Source: Tehran Agent: Jim

"Go ahead with the lesson as the London target would be the object of the lesson to be discussed at school."

This was from the transmission in Iran. The reply from Egypt was,

Message 1216hrs 113.786hz
Source: Cairo Agent: Jim
"Ok I will arrange for the pupils to go to school in a few days."

With a characteristic smile of content gleaming on his face Jim asked,
"Well Florie , to me that sounds like a definate plan for something , what do you think?"
After a due period of serious reflection Miss D'Arcy responded,
" I fully agree with you Jim. Something is being planned. I will arrange for this to take priority over all our other leads and also request that our MI6 agents in the field be updated and instructed to dig around in Cairo."
Miss D'Arcy then departed her office and made her way to the Director General's inner sanctum on the top floor of the 'doughnut' to fully update Sir Philip with all the facts thus far.
When Sir Philip Newman, a fifty-five year old , ex-

Government civil servant of many, many years standing, had sat and perused the translated messages and listened to the actions and suggestions from Miss D'Arcy immediately realised that he agreed with the possibility of an attack being planned against a target in the UK. To that effect he advised Florie of his intention to contact the NSA again but more importantly the Prime Minister of the UK.

With a sense of relief Florie returned to her office . Having gathered all her staff into the now somewhat crowded room she continued to inform them of the hightened alertness of the middle-east and for each of them who had contacts in Egypt and Iran to request their full attention.

With each and every mind now focussed the staff returned to their cubicles leaving Florie to again contact MI6 to request that all international agents be alerted and instructed to ferret around their middle-eastern haunts.

The air of frustration hung heavily throughout the 'doughnut' for the next few days as no further traffic ,signals or leads relating to the 'situation' was picked up. Nothing, not even a stiff from the network of MI6 agents.

Nothing.

Chapter Two

Fun and Games

Location: Hotel

The closer the party became the more uneasy Jim was within his skin. To this point his attention toward the beautiful Miss D'Arcy was purely cursory . At no time did he want to jeapordise his position within GCHQ over a broken or embarrasing relationship that went wrong with another member of staff, especially his boss so he kept a short distance but more importantly his lured thoughts to himself.

However, the celebration party would present a unique opportunity to release his guard and make an approach which if went wrong could easily be cast aside as an act made under the influence of alcohol.

His mind had been made up. The recent close activity of their working together over the middle-east transmissions had clearly provided the opportunity of an approach especially after having agreed to a dance or two.

It was now Friday 20th. The working day passed in a similar fashion to the previous few. Nothing happening except the odd call from Sir Philip to Miss D'Arcy anxious for news on any more transmissions. He too was being pressurised from above for news.

Jim cast his eyes to the middle of the ten clocks, displaying the relevant local times throughtout the world, which read 5.56pm. The relief from this particularly boring shift was so welcomed by Mr Norris as this would be his last sight of Miss D'Arcy before the party.

Gathering up his few belongings and neatly placing them into the brief case , Mr Norris strolled over to Miss D'Arcy's office and popped his head inside the open door,

"Goodnight Florie, see you tomorrow evening."

"Oh hi Jim. Yes goodnight and I look forward to that dance you promised me. Hope you didn't forget!"

Immediately on hearing that responce Jim's heartbeat rose a few beats.

This was looking positive he thought to himself as he walked to the exit door.

The majority of that evening Jim Norris spent preparing himself for the following day's performance which he felt could change his life for the better. His usual concentration to detail about his appearance became meticulous. Even the steam iron was thoroughly cleaned and polished before allowing it to press his best shirt, jacket and trousers. His best leather shoes gleemed like they were made of glass and that was just for the clothes. It was this perpetual attention to clinical and personal detail that was driving a wedge between him and Natalia, to the point that Natalia was too casting her net in search of a different catch.
As each day slid by their relationship saw the gap between them widening giving Norris's inclination towards his boss some degree of acceptability.
Saturday being the following day saw the ever hopeful Mr Norris pay a visit to the barbers for a tidy up of his locks and the purchase of some expensive after shave. If Natalia suspected anything, he would not worry. He really did feel that their relationship was already on a slippery slope.
On the other side of Cheltenham Florence D'Arcy was preening herself for the evening's activity. Her best red Jimmy Choo shoes were brought out of the cupboard to go with the new Karen Miller black number. Without doubt she too was a little excited.
The day soon passed with the evening sky darkening around 5.30pm.
With Natalia firmly advised by Jim Norris that the GCHQ celebration was for staff members only he made his way to the BMW patiently waiting outside the apartment. Selecting first he headed towards the Prestbury Road where he would turn right and drive towards the beautiful cotswold town of Winchcombe. After a couple of miles or so he spotted the signboard of the newly refurbished Ellenborough Park Hotel and prepared to turn into the drive. Jim had never taken the opportunity to visit the hotel since the improvements had been completed but was

well aware of what it was like beforehand. The old country house was huge and of a quality build , quietly sitting on the eastern perimeter of the famous Cheltenham race course.
Mr Norris recognised several of the parked cars denoting that he was not the first to arrive.
Miss D'Arcy's Audi TT coupe was nowhere to be seen.
"Hello Jim, good to see you" greeted Mr Norris as he exited his car.
"Oh good evening Brian. I see we are not the first then" Jim replied.
"Hope there is plenty of Champagne on tap" Brian continued as he headed for the front entrance of the hotel closely followed by the anxious Mr Norris.
The renovated interior of Ellenborough Park was most definately to Norris's satisfaction. His last recollection of the huge cotswold house was when he attended a conference several years previous and the drabe tired interior was all too obvious leaving a slightly depressed impression in his mind, but now, the varnished panelling, the refaced brickwork and deeply piled blue carpeting did much to eradicate his stored image.
"*GCHQ function is in the Race Room, down the hall and second on the right Sir"* directed the smartly dressed young lady on duty.
Immediately on entering the room Jim recognised most of the gathering including Sir Philip and the full board of Directors, but no Florence, as of yet.
The general mundane chit chat continued with the ocassional laugh being heard above the din. All the time Norris had one eye on the door hoping to catch a glimpse of Miss D'Arcy and then beeline for her before anyone else .
His patient observation worked as suddenley there stood the glamorous Florence in her little elegant black number. Immediately Jim departed his conversation with Brian and wove his way through the throng toward the door,

"Hi Florie, my you look so beautiful. Would you like a drink?"
"Good to see you Jim. I think I will have a Manhattan cocktail if possible please" she replied.
"Ok let's go to the bar and find out" Jim suggested.
Their conversation proceeded smoothly having started off with some general remarks about the office then gradually leading onto more personal matters until Brian strolled over from having finished his conversation with Sir Philip and asked Miss D'Arcy for a dance, which forced Jim into a situation of having to make a quick decision,
"After me Brian as Florie promised me the first and hopefully the second as well" looking Miss D'Arcy in the eye for a twinkle of agreement. The twinkle was evident. Jim took florie's hand and led her to the area boarded off for dancing, much to Brian's dismay.
The first two dances barely saw Norris more a muscle . The 'sixties' music just was not to his taste and could not get a rythem. He tried his best by schuffling his feet and waggling his arms but he was uncomfortable, unlike Miss D'Arcy who began to relax mainly under the influence of the two or was it three Manhattans!
Suddenly the the music changed to what used to be termed 'smoooch '. It was Florie that made the first move by gently moving in close to Norris and wrapping her arms around him,
"I think it's about time we danced properly, don't you Jim" she whispered in his ear.
His courage began to grow!
"Yes Florie."
Slowly but with a deliberate intention, in time with the vocals of the music, the two bodies glided across a section of the small prefabricated dance floor together. First one then two dances passed with neither aware of their colleagues around them. It was during the third dance, a

golden oldie sung by Andy Williams, that Florie upon missing a step allowed Jim's body to impinge closer to hers at which point she felt a rather hard object just below her tummy. Fully realising that Jim was showing more than mere interest in her and together with the copius amount of rye whiskey in her three manhattens, the usually shy Miss D'Arcy took the plunge by whispering into Jim's left ear,

"Should we book in for the night?"

Not wishing to display too much surprise, although in reality he could not believe his luck, the cool Mr Norris, with his hands gently resting on Florie's shoulders, gazed lustfully into Miss D'Arcy's deep brown eyes,

" Are you sure Florie? Could it not be difficult at work?"

"Fuck work Jim tomorrow is another day. Are you on?"

"Of course. Let's slip out of here quietly and check-in then" Norris suggested.

With a look of an anticipated surprise the young female Irish receptionist offered room 15 on the first floor.

"It is a quiet room overlooking the racecourse" she advised the couple.

Turning his head towards Miss D'Arcy,

"Yes that will be fine, thanks" Jim responded as he handed over his Barclaycard.

As they walked into the room Miss D'Arcy immediately walked over to the window and drew closed the heavy curtains before disappearing into the bathroom for a tidy up.

Still not quite fully realising his luck the nervous Mr Norris took advantage of this pregnant pause to remove his shoes and socks before pulling back the beautifully patterned bed cover. The scene was set with the thought of bedding the gorgeous Florie bringing a satisfied smile to his face then, before he could even remove his jacket in walked the sight of heaven from the bathroom.

Attired in just her tiny jet black panties and bra, the

handsome figure of Florie D'Arcy glided across the carpet straight into the arms of her night's conquest.
The kiss was deep and very French which Jim enjoyed so much after having dreamt of this moment for so long. The removal of his jacket whilst his tongue was tasting the sweet juices within her mouth proved ungainly and clumsy but somehow he managed it allowing it to drop to the floor.The slender female fingers with the maniculed nails roughly undid his tie encouraging Jim to then undo his shirt buttons in haste. The tie hit the floor and the free hands of Miss D'Arcy drew down his body and began to unfasten his trousers. Their hands touched as Jim undid the final shirt button. Zzzzzip as his trouser zip rapidly traversed to it's full travel, the trousers fell to Jim's feet exposing his pale blue boxers.
Smooching towards the bed the couple, still fully embraced, collapsed onto the soft mattress and began to embark on the act of passionate lovemaking.

Lying back on the white Egyptian cotton sheets the two naked, relaxing bodies began to loose their glistening complexion. Jim took hold of Miss D'arcy's hand,
"Are we ok? There's no going back now" he asked of his contented lover.
"Oh dear Jim. Of course we are ok. We are both intelligent adults who wanted the same thing. Come on let's do it again!" Florie cried out as she threw her slender body on top of his for a second helping.
Jim, whilst relishing the idea of a second cuming, struggled somewhat to get fully aroused with such a short interval but continued on as best he could.
It was the interruption of the strange polytone of Miss D'Arcy's smartphone gently vibrating on the bedside table that finally broke his concentration,
"Oh shit, not now" she muttered leaning over to observe the caller display.

"Oh god it's the doughnut Jim. I have better take it, sorry."
"No problem Florie" the relieved Norris informed her.
"Hello Dean. What's up?"
"Sorry to disturb you during your relaxing evening Miss D'Arcy but we have just intercepted some extremely disturbing conversation from the middle-east. You need to come in and see asap" Dean requested.
"Shit. Sorry Dean. Are you sure they are that important Dean?" she asked with a sense of frustration in her voice.
"Oh yes."
"Very well I will be there in twenty-five minutes" she advised him and went on to say to Jim,
"Maybe you had better come with me."
They quickly got dressed, departed the hotel and made for Florie's Audi.
"Leave your car here Jim and come with me. We can come back and pick up yours later" Miss D'Arcy insisted.
With it's characteristic whirr before starting the Audi TT burst into life. The main road was clear allowing Florie to pull out of the hotel drive without stopping. She hit forth gear swiftly bringing the speed up to fifty five miles per hour, fast enough for this stretch of road.
Unbeknown to her the continual changing of gear had allowed her dress to ride high up her leg giving Jim a bird's eye view of her slender thigh. The temptation was too much. He had to put his right hand on her leg and slide it upwards.
"Enjoying that Jim?" she asked.
"Of course."
"Then feel free to go further" Florie suggested as a delicate wetness began to creep between her legs and with her driving concentration lowering itself in a direct ratio to the raising of her estrogen level. She failed to see the traffic light glowing red as the Audi flashed over the Cheltenham Boy's College junction narrowly missing contact with a

Ford Mondeo.
"Careful Florie, that was close!" Jim uttered.
It was the reflection of the blue flashing light in her overhead mirror that suddenly gained her attention which in turn instinctively guided her car to a controlled stop.
Lowering her window the officer whom she vaguely knew, presented himself,
"Miss D'Arcy are you aware that you drove through a red light back there?"
"Oh hi there. Yes I do now but I am in a hurry to get to a meeting at GCHQ and did not see it at the time" she responded.
The odour of alcohol eminating from the car's interior was all to obvious to the officer as he listened to her excuse.
"Would you mind blowing in this bag please as I have reason to suspect that you have been drinking miss" he continued.
"Yes I have had a couple but I got this extremely urgent call from HQ. I have to go now. It is a matter of National importance."
"That may be so but.." before he could finish,
"Look I do not have the time for this officer. The country might well be under a terroristic threat. I need to get there NOW! Do you understand?" she insisted.
"Very well Miss D'Arcy I have no choice but to believe you. Follow me I will give you an escort to the main gates of GCHQ" the officer suggested as he sped back to his panda car.
The Audi set off once again down the Gloucester Road keeping pace with the police car, with it's strobing rooftop blue light clear for all to see.
"OMG that was a close shave Florie" Jim pointed out.
"A woman's charm Jim. Works everytime!"

As the main security gates opened, Miss.D'Arcy purported a gesture of thanks to the departing police car and entered

the compound.
Immediately they both burst through the office door there sat Dean listening intently in on the headsets who gestured the couple to sit next to him and read the transcripts thus far received. At this point a further transmission had just been intercepted with Dean writing down the english translation of the arabic he was overhearing. He, like most of the senior operators, were that good at instant translation.
Taking the top message Miss D'Arcy, with Jim overlooking her shoulder, began to read the english version of the first message which had been calculated to have eminated from Iran,

Message One. 21/9/13 1623hrs. 113.786hz
Source: Tehran Agent: Dean

"School approved to open in London seven days from today. Advise the teacher and his students to prepare for term start. All arrangements are approved."

Then Miss D'Arcy turned to the second message translation which appeared to be the reply from Cairo,

Message Two. 21/9/13 1710hrs. 113.786hz
Source: Cairo Agent: Dean

"We will inform all concerned and contact the teacher immediately ."

"Please fetch me a coffee Dean whilst I read the other messages" Florie asked as she drew her chair closer to the desk and began looking at message three.

Message Three. 21/9/13 1943hrs 95.62hz
Source: Cairo Agent: Dean

"Teacher, we have been given the go ahead for school to start in seven days."

Message Four 21/9/13 2043hrs 95.62hz
Source: Damascus Agent: Dean

"I understand. I will conclude the research and execute the opening as we discussed. The pupils will be dispatched within 48hrs.

Miss D'Arcy continued reading with deep concern.

Message Five: 21/9/13 2123hrs 95.62hz
Source: Cairo Agent: Dean

"Do you have all the frequencies, timetable and codes?"

Message Six: 21/9/13 2142hrs 95.62hz
Source: Damascus Agent: Dean

"Yes. "

Taking a few seconds to totally digest the contents of all the messages, Miss D'Arcy took to her feet and asked all three to immediately gather in her office.
"Ok we have all read the transmissions. What are your ideas? Dean?" Florie asked.
"*Well I think an attack on UK is definately planned. By referring to timetables it could be trains or buses ..."*
"Or planes!" Jim interrupted.
"I agree with Jim. Planes seem most likely especially when frequencies are also mentioned" ventured Miss D'Arcy.
After a more lengthy discussion it was agreed that Miss

D'Arcy would immediately request the return of Sir Philip for an update.

Chapter Three

The Plot Thickens

Location: Damascus

It took President Akbari a few minutes to read and digest the transcripts from his Egyptian conterpart, President Kalesh. The arrangements for the pupils in school coding was that the Egyptian Brotherhood, now feeling the threat of revolution from within their own people from the covert stirrings of western implants, had now sanctioned the release of Al-Mawla (signifying ..The Protectors) agents, now securely embedded in the anti-Government regimes in Syria, to travel to UK and ensure the planned operation strikes maximum collateral damage to the UK and attracts publicity.
The various factions of Al-Mawla had ferreted their way into various Syrian revolutionary groups fighting, with almost no weapons, against the barbaric antics of Assad's Government troops. Their journey over the mountains from Afghanistan, over the sea from Somalia and over the desert from Mali took months of arduous travel for the fundamentalist fighters who saw the worsening situation in Syria as a brilliant platform of opportunity from which to vent their hatred towards the west by integrating with the Syrian rebels thus confusing and embarressing any possible military aid from the west. Then of course should the rebels eventually be successful and overthrow President Assad then they, Al-Mawla, would be in a position to claim or take territory for their help thus providing a safe and secure foothold from which to further their cause, right in the centre of the middle-east.
Abasin Zadran, (codenamed The Teacher) the self appointed fundamentalist leader of the Al-Mawla forces in Syria was a clever man. Having been educated in Cairo University he was well versed in human strategy and as a

dedicated Muslim and an ardent believer in every word of the Qur'an had come up with this plan , this extraordinary plan to tap into the NATS (National Air Traffic Services) aviation computers that service London's Heathrow airport and alter some of the vital settings that incoming pilots require. Zadran and his learned contacts, following exhaustive research, had found a way to hack into the ILS (Instrument Landing System) computer system at Heathrow and without even having to leave Syria could, at will, change any of the default parameters or alter computer settings within an incoming aircraft.
By switching through several other computer stations located in friendly countries, this remote cyber attack would leave no trace back to Zadran's home laptop in Damascus.
Within the next couple of days he would issue instructions for the Syrian rebel leader to contact his United Nations allies and demand that arms be immediately supplied to them to assist in their strife against Assad or failing that to launch an all out attack on Assad's forces. In the event of neither demand being exceeded too then one of the UN countries would face some uncomfortable consequences. Whatever the west decided Zadran felt in total control and would do well in all the options.

If and when the UK attack, which he inwardly knew would happen, was successfully completed Zadran felt safe in the knowledge that he could see no way for the UK security services to trace the viral source directly back to him which would leave him free to continue with other plans presently sitting in the back of his mind. The fallout from the disaster he had for Heathrow would hit the headlines the world over. It was to be big and bold, however once NATS had established the vulnerability of their systems to a cyber attack following the disaster they would no doubt improve the firewalls and defence security etc which meant that this

present attack would have to be the first and last so Zadran would have to make it memorable!
Over the past four/five months Zadran had recruited and trained two trusted Egyptian colleagues, sharing the same beliefs as his own, to travel to England posing as tourists which they could easily arrange with their nationality and to locate themselves in strategic points around Heathrow airport on the day of the attack to inform Zadran of the appearance of the main intended target and if circumstances allow, a secondary and if luck prevailed a third target. They were also to record with a camcorder the whole attack, from beginning to end, from the safety of the perimeter of the airport in order for Zadran and his fellow fundalmentalists in Egypt and Iran to have a true record of their strike at the west which might later be used in their recruitment and propaganda programmes.
The two on site selectees would also report back on the progress of the media and press reports that would inevitably be shown on British TV following the attack . Zadran, Akbari and Kalesh would all be glued to 'you tube' to observe first hand the various reports as they fed onto the internet site.

As the two agents left the shelter, buried deep in the rubble of a north eastern suburb of Damascus, to make their way to the train station to commence the arduous journey to London via Turkey and Bulgaria from where they would take a flight to Brussels and from there embark on the Eurostar train to central London, Zadran began to make arrangements to meet up with Asphan Rachid within the next three to four days to discuss the final installation of the computer with it's dedicated software, specially written for this attack by some learned Al-Mawla geek from Cairo when **Booom**!. as yet another of Assad's shells burst in the house on the other side of the street bringing it down to the ground in an almighty cloud of dust. Zadran's

underground HQ felt the vibration bringing plaster and dust cascading down from the ceiling covering the terrorist in a greyish powder. Fortunately only light debris fell on the closed laptop computer causing only superficial stratches. Immediately though, as a double check, Zadran opened up the Sony Vaio and depressed the starter button. Within seconds the windows 7 picture sprang to life confirming the laptop to still be fully functionable. With a breath of relief he then activated the shut down procedure and closed the lid to await the arrival of the courier who was to go and see Asphan with his instructions for a meeting.
Running in like a frightened cat as he tried to dodge the occasional bullet and fallout debris, the courier finally arrived in the basement of the now almost derilect building, *"Salaam Abasin you wanted to see me?"* he uttered.
Turning to gaze upon the breathless young courier Zadran spoke,
"Yes. Go to Asphan and tell him to be here at 11 o'clock on Wednesday morning for final briefing and tell him to bring the codes."
"The codes?"
"Yes the codes he will understand. Do not fail my friend" Zadran confirmed.
"Very well Abasin consider it done" and off the courier ran back up the stairs and into the war torn street.

Boom!! as another shell landed in the centre of the road bombarding the adjacent buildings with yet another broadside of debris. This time the shock wave traversed into the house and down into the basement knocking the Egyptian Zadran to the ground. Fortunately the Sony laptop remained steadfast on the table but for good measure as soon as he got his breath back Zadran transferred the laptop to a safer location in the floor safe.

At this point with so many shells being suddenly targeted at the street above he was becoming extremely concerned for the safety of his Headquarters.

Then he remembered the courier: was he caught in that explosion? Gathering his strength Zadran ran up the stairs and out into the street and gazed in the easterly direction only to see the courier limping as he turned into the next street .. he was alive and heading in the correct direction. *"Thank's be to Allah!"* Zadran muttered to himself as he returned to the relative safety of the basement.
All he could do now was to hope that Assad's fire would be directed eleswhere and soon.

Chapter Three

A nervous wait

Location: GCHQ

Having received such an implicit request from a senior manager such as Miss D'Arcy for him to return to the 'Doughnut' , Sir Philip , having made his apologies to his wife, departed the festivities with haste, had entered the Middle-East section to find Miss D'Arcy and her team patiently awaiting his arrival.
"Good evening Sir. Sorry to drag you away but we have some dramatic developments in the Middle East. Dean has just intercepted all this" as she handed him the transcripts, *"And I feel that you will need to contact the Prime Minister, Sir"* Florie informed Sir Philip.
Taking up the nearest chair, Sir Philip sat down and very carefully read through the messages, at least three times.
"So what is your team's final conclusion Miss D'Arcy" he asked.
"*Well Sir, it is our, and most definately my, conclusion that a terrorist attack on possibly an airport in the UK will take place on the 28th of this month."*
Giving a second's digestion Sir Philip stood up,
"I agree with you all and will contact the PM right away, meanwhile bring in all your operatives and carefully monitor all transmissions from the middle-east for more clues ...well done to you all. Miss D'Arcy will you come with me please."
Sir Philip, with the transcripts in hand, departed with Florie to his office on the top floor to call the PM direct on the official hotline.
This was the first time that Miss D'Arcy had entered the boss's inner sanctum and found the surroundings rather plush ..so totally different from her usual working environment.

"Take a seat Miss D'Arcy and be prepared to speak to the PM if he requests."
Composing his thoughts for a couple of seconds Sir Philip lifted the red receiver and depressed the sole button on the keyboard. A somewhat strange dialling tone was clearly heard by Miss D'Arcy , even at the ten feet distance she was from the phone. This was the scrambling interrogation enacting itself.
Suddenly a voice was heard,
"Morrison here."
"Mr Prime Minister, Philip Newman here. Sorry to disturb you but we may have an incident about to happen sufficiently bad for me to suggest a COBRA meeting for 0900hrs tomorrow with your attendance, in Downing St. May I have your sanction for that, Sir?" Sir Philip stated.
"0900hrs, are you really certain of the importance of the situation Newman as I will have to cancel a Cabinet meeting to attend?" the Prime Minister asked.
"Yes Sir."
"Very well 0900 it is at No.10" and put down the receiver.
Newman stood up and addressed Miss D'Arcy,
"I want you and your select team downstairs to be there as well and be prepared to give a full account of the situation to the board. Bring along twenty copies of these transcripts which I want you to deligate as 'Top Secret'. On no account is anyone outside of the team working on this project to be informed as to what is going on. Do you fully understand?"
"Yes Sir. We will see you at 0900hrs" Miss D'Arcy stated and departed back to join her two companions in the Middle East section.
Both were sat, headsets on, concentrating on their displays as Florie walked in,
"Gentlemen we are all to be at Downing St. tomorrow at 0900hrs for a briefing to COBRA (Cabinet Office Briefing

Room A . The emergency response team for national emergencies). I will call in a night team to keep watch so you had both go home for some shut eye and I will meet you both here at 0700hrs and take us all to London in my car. Jim a quick word in my office."
"Wow Florie Downing St. That will be nice" spoke Jim.
"This is extremely important Jim so I want you to go to your home and not mine and get some sleep meanwhile I will take you back to the hotel to collect your car. Come on let's go." she commanded.

At 0655hrs the next morning all three, Miss D'Arcy, Jim and Dean, gathered in the GCHQ car park and somchow managed to squeeze into the small Audi TT 2+2. The six foot Dean was not too pleased to be renegated to the poor excuse for rear seating but being the junior in rank he had too suffer.
The journey by way of the A40 to Oxford and then onto the M40 took them into the Paddington area of central London. Florie then followed the signs for the Edgware Road which eventually brought them to Park Lane and the Wellington Arch. Before entering Constitution Hill Florie asked for the timc to which Dcan answcrcd,
"0843."
"Bit tight but then the traffic is heavier than I anticipated" stated Miss D'Arcy.
Buckingham Palace passed by on their right as the Audi drove into The Mall. Within minutes they were through Trafalgar Square and heading down Whitehall.
"There it is Florie just after the Cenotaph. Where are you going to park?" asked Jim who was now beginning to get butterflies in his stomach.
"Going to try in Downing Street itself if possible, after all this is a national emergency."
As the Audi drew up in front of the large, imposing, black security gates one of the selected policemen raised his

hand,
"Good morning Madam. Sorry but you cannot stop here" he said in a grumpy voice.
With the electric window lowered Miss D'Arcy flashed her GCHQ I/D card at the policeman,
"It's ok officer we are expected for the COBRA meeting in No.10. I see Sir Philip Newman's Bentley has already arrived."
A quick check of the authorised personnel due to be admitted that morning, written in his notebook, soon found the names of the three passengers tallied.
"That's ok Miss D'Arcy you may go in" the policeman beckoned as he signalled to his colleague to open the gates.
With the car safely parked outside No.11 they walked to the famous black door of No.10 to be greeted by the smartly dressed commissionaire.
"Florence D'Arcy and team for the COBRA meeting" Miss D'Arcy advised him.
"Please go through into the Cabinet Room down the hall to your right" he advised.
The short walk down the hallway took all of ten seconds before entering the main Cabinet Office through the solid mahogony double entrance doors. The sight of the famous twin columns and elaborate panelling was somewhat overwhelming for Mr Norris as he gazed around the room.
"Ah there you are Miss D'Arcy just in the nick of time. Come in all of you and sit over there on that side of the table next to The Police Commissioner" greeted Sir Philip at which point in walked the familiar plump figure of Dennis Morrison, the Prime Minister, closely followed by The Home Secretary.
"Ladies and Gentlemen, good morning to you all. Please be seated" advised the PM.
When all were settled and the last of the domestic staff had left the PM called the meeting to order,

"Ok I have convened this special meeting this morning on the suggestion of Sir Philip Newman, who as you know is the Director General of GCHQ down there in Cheltenham so I will hand over to him for an explanation of the situation.... Philip."

"Thankyou Mr Prime Minister. Last night it was brought to my attention by Miss D'Arcy, over there, that we have intercepted what can be classified as a grade 1 threat. The intercepted messages were from Syria, Egypt and Iran and appear to confirm a terroristic act upon one of our airports on the 28th of this month. I have here copies of the interceptions for your guidance and suggest they do not ever leave this room. I will now hand you over to Miss Florence D'Arcy who will provide you with the latest intel."
Florence took to her feet,
"I am the Senior Manager of the Middle-East section of GCHQ and having received all the transcripts of the intercepted telephone conversations from Tehran, Cairo and Damascus I convened a crisis meeting with my two colleagues here present. I might add that only us three ,plus Sir Philip, from GCHQ are aware of the FULL content of these messages. It is our considered opinion that London's Heathrow Airport will be the target of a terrorist act on the 28th. That is the limit of our knowledge thus far." Florence then sat down. Immediately Lesley Billington, The Police Commissioner, asked,
"Have you no idea of the people involved?"
"No, none" answered Miss D'Arcy.
There was a stunned silence of a few seconds before the PM asked Ms Jessica Billgate-Hardman (Head of MI6 and more commomly known as 'B' for boss) whether she had any intel from any of her agents in Damascus and Cairo. There was none.

"Ok then" the PM continued,*" in view of the lack of intel we will treat this as an imminent threat so I will instruct the Defence Secretary to take the appropriate actions at Heathrow. Lesley will you arrange to take into custody all known suspects in the London area and Jessica put all your middle east agents on full alert. My office will contact the airline bosses and fill them in. I will not order the closure of the airport for the 28th as this could start a panic and would achieve nothing in the long run. We will all meet here on the 26th for a final update"* the PM announced and closed the meeting.
With the PM gone the Home Secretary quietly made her way over to the GCHQ trio and introduced herself,
"We are all very grateful for your alertness and would ask you to be even more alert for the next few days but you surely must have a gut feeling as to who might be behind this threat?"
"Well ...." Jim started to say before Florie interrupted,
"It would be imprudent to say anything at this stage ma'am as we really have no clue."
"No let him continue" spoke Fiona.
"Well I have long thought that the Egyptian terrorist Zadran could be in Damascus ..maybe he is behind this. It's just a gut feeling Ma'am" Jim continued.
"I appreciate your frankness Mr Norris and in view of this are you able to speculate as to the type of act he could be planning?" the Home Secretary went on to ask.
"No except to say it will be bad!"
"Why do you say that Mr Norris?"
"Well, at least the Foreign Secretary and you should be aware that since the demise of Bin-Datan both the frequency and scale of terroristic attacks throughout the world have intensified and that this extremist Zadran is plying for the top vacancy in Al-Mawla. One big attack

would surely set him on that pedestal ..or so he might think" continued Jim.
Immediately Miss D'Arcy intervened,
"Jim I did not realise that you were so well informed."

"Ah well Florie there's a lot you are not aware of!"
"Enough. Keep your agency on it's toes and keep me informed directly on this number" as she handed Miss D'Arcy her personal card. *"For sake of time I want you to by-pass Sir Philip and liase direct with me. Is that understood!"*
"Yes" came from Miss D'Arcy.
Mrs. Campbell (The Home Secretary) then left the room.
It was at this point, having observed the Home Secretary talking to his group, that Sir Philip made his way to the GCHQ trio anxious to find out what was said,
"What was that all about Miss D'Arcy?"
Not wishing to become a pawn in some political game Florie quickly replied,
"Nothing much sir. She just wished us luck in listening out for more transmissions ..that's all" as a pale blushness crept over her face. Sir Philip being an old hand in the art of body language, immediately knew she was bending the truth but in the interests of the short time to the 28th he was prepared to cast aside any further worries as to why this might be,
"Very well, you had all better get back to Cheltenham and set up a 24hr watch on all known frequencies and networks with as many staff as you can. Meanwhile I will liase with the NSA in Washington and enlist their resources for any leads. I look forward to a progress update tomorrow afternoon Miss D'Arcy."
" Very well. Goodbye sir."
Once again the trio crammed into the Audi and prepared themselves for the reverse journey home to Cheltenham.
Meanwhile all hell had broken out across Whitehall in the

Ministry of Defence as the Defence Secretary, Alistar Bennet, had just been contacted by the Home Secretary to set up a military defence shield, in the form of discreetly armed checkpoints around Heathrow Airport within the next few days. The panic that Mr. Bennet had was that he had just ordered a large contingent of troops and equipment to Afghanistan to counteract a recent Taliban advance and that he would struggle to provide enough reserve troops and armoured cars for a Heathrow operation. After all the perimeter of Heathrow was almost ten miles with at least five individual entrances but most of all it had some two hundred and fifty thousand people working there and twenty thousand vehicle movements per day.

He would have to bring in the relatively untrained Territorial Army. This would take time and a mammoth amount of effort. Aside from all of that he could not ignore the possibility that the sight of armed troops at a major UK airport would set off a panic especially with the press coverage that would undoubtedly ensue. However he would endeavour to do his best as usual.

The same onset of mild panic also hit Police Commissioner Billington as she was also suffering from a manpower cutback from the recent cuts in her expenditure budget so she would have to cancel all forthcoming leave for the Metropolitan Division and draw in reserves from other nearby forces. A close liason with Alistar Bennet would have to be a priority.

The **"European Photo-Book** "collection

Chapter Four

Last Minute Fears

As Zadran, sat behind the remains of what could have been called a desk, casually glanced at his watch, it read
11:26am. No Asphan. The last few hours had seen a marked reduction in the shelling of the Barzeh area of Damascus which gave the Egyptian born terrorist cause for hope that his colleague Asphan, a Yemeni dissident, would be on time ...maybe the courier did not get through the barrage and relay the message ...maybe Asphan had been killed. All these thoughts ran through Zadran's head. He was becoming nervous as without the computer skills of his colleague the attack on Heathrow Airport could not go ahead and his standing within Al-Mawla would not be raised.
11: 38am came and went, when suddenly Zadran heard a cough followed by footsteps on the broken stairs,
"Abasin, Abasin are you there" a voice cried out.
"Yes I'm here is that you Asphan?"
"Yes, Salaam Abasin. Sorry for my late arrival but I got caught in a firefight about a kilometre back " spoke the out of breath Asphan as hc entered the basement, walked over to his friend and kissed him on both cheeks.
"Thanks be to Allah that you made it. Now to business" Zadran advised.
Following an extensive examination of the laptop and checking that the wi-fi broadband connection was still in tact Asphan, the dissident from a Sana'a birth who had been a recognised writer of computer software before the Syrian civil war, began to log onto various sites to test the download speed. Everything seemed ok.

Satisfied by the Sony's performance Asphan then requested that Zadran ran through precisely what he wanted him to do as at this time Asphan only knew that he was to enter

the network of a foreign country and tinker with a programme.
With a somewhat dusty cup of coffee in one hand and a half smoked cigarette in the other, Zadran continued with the outlining of his deadly plan.

Now fully familiar with the details Asphan called for a cup of coffee and a little thinking time to calculate the intricacies of such a complex cyber attack. The one thing he was certain of was that the corei3 processor in the Sony would not be sufficiently fast for such a hack and that a wi-fi connection would not be stable enough to carry the instructions without a break-up of the signal, so whilst his friend was in the other room, engaged in brewing a fresh coffee, Asphan quickly picked up Zadran's mobile phone which he observed lying on the desk earlier and called his brother on the other side of Damascus,
"Salaam Arid, it is Asphan. Now listen do you have a core i9 processor and a twenty metre broadband lead available?"
"Yes I think so."
" Good Keep them handy and I will pick them up this afternoon. Salaam."
In walked Zadran with coffee in hand completely unaware that his mobile phone has just been activated.
"Well Asphan, have you thought how to do this thing?"
Following a considerable pause to take a couple of mouthfuls of coffee and fully complete his intellectual thoughts the young Asphan replied,
"Yes, I think so . I can easily enter the NATS computer and alter the glide slope parameters of their ILS but an even better idea would be to use the ILS signal to piggy-back my signal to enter the aircraft's own computers and select the autopilot to follow the corrupted glideslope. If I also instruct a by-pass of the manual autopilot cutout then the pilots could not switch off their autopilot computer! How

about that Abasin?"

Stunned with admiration of the capability and ingenuity of his Yemeni friend Zadran responded,
"You can do that!"
"Of course and not only that as Heathrow has two runways I can corrupt both ILS's so you could take out two aircraft" Asphan continued with pride in his voice not realising that the second runway would be for take-offs.
"This is pure genius my friend but to push your skills a little bit further can you select a particular aircraft to crash?"
Asphan thought for a second,
"If you can provide me with the exact time that the aircraft is approaching it's landing, then yes. Can you do that?"
Zadran smiled,
"Yes I can do that as I will have a couple of operatives at the airport who can relay when the plane is sight directly to me."
"That sounds good. I will need at least thirty seconds to input the data once I have confirmation of the aircraft" Asphan informed Zadran.
"Ok I will instruct the operatives to base themselves as far out as possible to give you that thirty seconds Asphan."
Now that the details and procedures required to carry out this deadly assault on a British aircraft had been worked out both agreed to meet back at the HQ basement at 0500hrs on the 28th , fully prepared to engage the cyber attack. Asphan departed to make his way to his brothers house.

It was now time for Zadran to contact Ahmed, the established leader of the official Syrian rebel army and instruct him to make his demand to the United Nations to immediately supply his army with a great deal of sofisticated weapons and ammunition or suffer the consequences. There was no expectation that the UN would concur but the denial would serve as the catalyst for the attack on Heathrow.

* * *

The silence of the Middle East section was suddenly broken as Dean, the ever observant operator, cried out,
"I have him, I have him on 95.62hz!"
Immediately Dean switched on the back-up recorder as a double measure and activated the auto print out. Both Jim and a couple of the other operators gathered round Dean's console anxious for a readout of the transcript. They would have to wait as Florence would be the first to be told.
Several minutes passed in the hope of a further message or reply being heard but none came ..that was it! With the printout in hand Dean and Jim rushed into Florie's office and placed it on her desk.
With Dean and Jim patiently standing in front of the desk Miss D'Arcy read out the English transcript of the Egyptian message,

Message one. (Originator) 25/9/13 0954hrs 95.62hz
Source : Damascus Agent: Dean

"Salaam Arid, it is Asphan now listen. Do you have a corei9 processor and a twenty metre broadband lead available?"

Message Two (Reply) 25/9/13 0955hrs unknown
Source: Damascus Agent: Dean

"Yes I think so."

Message Three (Originator) 25/9/13 0957hrs 95.62hz
Source: Damascus Agent: Dean

"Good keep them handy and I will pick them up this afternoon, Salaam."

Florie examined the details and compared them with the previous set that had been distributed at the COBRA meeting and realised the frequenceny of one of the phones was consistant ..95.62hz. This was indeed the same source eminating in Damascus, Syria.
Both Jim and Dean remained silent awaiting the responce from their manager. The wait was all of thirty seconds,
"Very well I concur that the first message was from the same mobile phone unit but the layout of the words leads me to suggest it was not the same caller! If I am right then we have a cell at work not an individual ..this is bad. Would either of you agree with me?"
The brains of the two males could be heard ticking over,
"Yes" they both agreed.
"Ok then this Asphan and Arid must be part of that cell which accounts for at least three" Miss D'Arcy continued.
"Now what could be the significance of a core i9 processor and broadband lead?" she asked.
Dean being the computer specialist immediately offered some information,
"A core i9 is an extremely modern and fast processor which would suggest to me that the computer they have is not fast enough for a particular programme and the lead could be for a more stable and lengthy upload from a wi-fi set. Afterall Damascus is a war zone and a wi-fi signal could not be guaranteed to function without any interference of break."

"Now that is what I call Geek thinking Dean. Well done" commended Florie.
Jim then ventured his opinion,
"If you put this intelligence alongside the mention of timetables and frequencies from the other transcripts then it could cleary indicate to me that the target is most definately an airport." To which Dean added,
"I agree but which one? If a cyber hack is being undertaken it could be any airport or even more than one!"
Without any further discussion Florence announced that she was going to call the MI6 and MI5 boys and get them down to GCHQ that afternoon for a crisis meeting and in the meanwhile would give The Home Secretary an update as ordered.

At Heathrow Airport the sight of military armoured cars was begining to be noticed by the general public as the reference tweets on Twitter were rising by the hour. One of the most valuable sources of local intel for GCHQ was Twitter so the increase in traffic with reference to the military build up around Heathrow was giving concern.
Mr Alistar Bennet (Defence Secretary) was begining to feel between a rock and a hard place. On one hand he had to be seen to be counteracting the terrorist threat that as yet the public were unaware of, but on the other not to panic the population or affect the revenues of the airlines especially in the absence on any concrete evidence that Heathrow was to be the target. Sleepless night's up to the 29th were to be on the cards for Mr. Bennet and his colleagues.

Jessica Billgate-Hardman, a rather hard looking thirty five year old female with short auburn hair, was the first to arrive shortly followed by the dashing forty two year old Etonian Kevin McCloud (MI5). With their high

classification of security neither had difficulty in being admitted into the building but nevertheless had to be shown to Miss D'Arcy's office by a commissionaire, who politely knocked on the door,
" Excuse me Miss D'Arcy I have this lady and Gentleman who say they have an appointment with you."
The first to speak was Mrs Billgate-Hardman,
"Good Afternoon Miss D'Arcy I am Jessica Hardman (not quoting her full name as she deemed it inappropriate at this level of meeting) *of MI6 and this is Kevin McCloud , Senior Controller of MI5 Terror Threat section"* spoke Mrs Hardman as she entered the office.
"Do come in, coffee?"
Both said yes.
"Before continuing I want to call in my two colleagues who are most involved in this affair .... Jim and Dean, please come in here," she yelled from the office door.
Following the introductory formalities Florence formerly convened the meeting by activating the voice recorder.
She first outlined the intel so far intercepted by GCHQ to the two agents who agreed that an airport was to be a cyber target on the 28th. Miss D'Arcy then continued,
"Mrs. Hardman do you have contacts/agents in Damascus?"
"Yes" she replied.
"Then can you instruct them to concentrate all their activities on the Barzeh area of north east Damascus as this is the approximate area where the 95.62hz transmissions eminated. They should be looking for a high speed computer with broadband connection. The terrorists Abasin Zadran, Asphan and another called Arid are the names to search for and also as a long shot could you concentrate your agents in Tehran and Cairo just in case they might hear of anything" Miss D'Arcy instructed.
"No problem I will signal all three agents immediately."
Florence then turned to Mr. McCloud,

"What are you gut instincts as to which airport might be the target?"
"I have to say Heathrow as the first then Birmingham and Glasgow, possibly Gatwick. I say those as all four have major National carriers flying into them. You have American Airlines, United Airlines, British Airways, Air France and El-Al all of which would present a juicy target with their countries emblem clearly written on the aircraft's exterior and all represent an enemy to an Islamic terrorist. However if they are intending on a cyber attack then it will be almost impossible to stop them unless we knew the precise category 'B' (Mrs Hardman) *that's where any intel from your agents could help."*
The meeting broke up.

* * *

In Cairo the political situation took a turn for the worse. The Brotherhood's President Kalesh, having been deposed by the Army in the recent Coup D'etat, had received no response for his plea for help from either the British or the Americans which provoked him into agreeing to supply backing to the ' Teacher' in the first place, was informed that he was to go on public trial for treason. As this revelation fed down to his followers on the street another revolution was being kindled. Within hours of the official trial announcement, Tahrir Square in central Cairo gradually became a battlefield with bricks, blocks of concrete, bottles and tear gas being thrown by both sides. Several British and American flags could be clearly seen on fire as the angered crowd set light to them in protest of no response for help.

The angered General, temporarily in charge of Egyptian affairs grew anxious at the violence and immediately

ordered the incarceration of Ex-President Kalesh thus, not knowingly, depriving him of any further direct contact with his friends in Tehran and Damascus.
Zadran was now on his own and uncontactable should any change of plan be required from either Tehran or Cairo!

* * *

Barring any unforseen calamities the attack on Heathrow was on for the 28th!

Chapter Five

The Pressue Builds

Thursday the 26th came and went with the COBRA meeting having reached no further however down at GCHQ without any undue echo traffic being picked up from either Damascus or Cairo which gave Jim and Florie an ample excuse to spend several hours together, either in her office when they portrayed the scene of working together on the case or carefully sneeking out for a coffee break , ostensibly to the canteen but actually disappearing into the normally deserted computer server room for a quick bit of roly-poly. Despite being the professionals that there were their carnal instinct could not be contained!

It was now around 4:40pm as Jim calmly walked back into the operations room followed some five minutes later by Miss D'Arcy who was wearing her haircomb on the opposite side to when she had departed.. The standard of intellect and mental awareness employed by GCHQ was extremely high so the attempt at hiding their antics did nothing than highlight their activity from the remainder of the staff. It, however, seemed to provide some light relief in the office from the stress of the present situation.

The external telephone ran in Miss D'Arcy's office making her run to answer it,

"Hello Florence D'Arcy here" she answered in a heavy breath.

A rather posh voice came through the receiver,

"Hello Miss D'Arcy, Jessica Hardman. Are we on a secure line?"

"*Oh* yes"

"*Good. I have a little intel for you. Since the COBRA meeting this morning we've picked up a suspect in Damascus who, with a little persuasion, has confirmed that Zadran is definately in Damascus and Asphan Rachid is a known computer software expert. Unfortunately the suspect died before telling us any more. Hope this helps you as it tells us nothing of quality.*"

"It could help, thanks Jessica" and replaced the receiver before rushing out to advise Jim Norris and Dean.
This information was of great help to GCHQ as it confirmed that the prophecies of both Jim and Dean seemed to add up, in that the known terrorist Zadran was planning an attack and that it would involve a computer cyber attack of some description. Now they had sufficient concrete evidence to approach all the major National airline Directors at Heathrow, Gatwick, Birmingham and Glasgow airports to advice that they monitor their computers with added guile.
Over the next couple of hours this is exactly what Miss D'Arcy did over the telephone. At this stage, with only a day to go before the intended attack, Miss D'Arcy saw no time left to visit the airline boards personally so felt there was nothing to loose by contacting them via an open landline. Was that a mistake ..maybe we will never know!
In the event the warning may have been to no avail as each airline director in turn, except for United Airlines who was to consider cancelling all it's UK bound flights for the 28th, responded with a similar attitude ...what more could they do to protect themselves with only 24hrs to go without creating an enormous panic amongst passengers and of course their own staff let alone punch a dent in their meagre profits! They all promised though to upgrade their vigilance on passenger security at check-in in the hope that any suspect carrying an electronic device, such as a mobile phone, laptop computer, i-pad etc, would voluntarily allow it to be placed in the hold of the aircraft and not in the cabin. Those that refused would be searched and questioned further with a denial of boarding being held as a final option for that passenger.
Somewhat dismayed and concerned with these responces Florence then took it upon herself to also contact the

Airport Authorites through the BAA (British Airport Aurthority) but it now being way past 7:00pm found it impossible to get hold of anyone in authority.

Now she was getting frustated so in the event called up Fiona Campbell (Home Secretary) and updated her with her own frustration. Mrs. Campbell had the final power to locate the authories at their home which she proceeded to do with the utmost vigor.
Again the responce from Sir Bernard, the Chairman of BAA, was of little succour. Time was just too short to carry out any major changes to any computer systems and the question of cost and disruption was not inconsiderable especially as Sir Bernard pointed out to the Home Secretary that threats like this are received quite regularly and none to date had turned out to be genuine.
Like Miss D'Arcy, Fiona Campbell began to elude frustration in her behaviour..what else could she do! Should the attack prevail and turn out to be successful ,then all fingers would be pointed at her for an explanation. She was not prepared to fall on her own sword, as did several other Cabinet Ministers of late, in the event of a disaster so she wanted every avenue and eventuality that befell her responsibility to be well and truel covered. To this regard she had recorded all her conversations with the airlines and authorities and safely tucked away the CD in her personal safe.

After much consideration over the last couple of days there was no doubt in her mind that this cyber attack upon a major UK airport was going to take place resulting in a national disaster and she was determined to protect her position in Cabinet. It had taken years and years of hard work and sacrificies to attain this exulted position and she was not going to lose it because of someone elses lackadaisical attitude.

The same attitude could be applied to that of Miss D'Arcy who was also convinced of the forthcoming attack.
Both women had overcome the male bastion bureaucracy to attain their status and neither were going to be defeated!
It was getting late so Florie decided to call it a day and go home for a meal and a good rest and refreshen for the next day which was the 27th!
As she walked through the section Jim caught sight and instantly ran in her direction,
"Florie where are you going. I finish my shift in a few minutes so can't you wait and we can out for a dinner together."
"Not tonight Jim. I have too much pressure at the moment and we will both will need to be fresh tomorrow. You go home now as well and I will see you in the morning. goodnight" and continued to the exit door.

* * *

The following morning was the beginning of a pleasant day, for the weather at least, as Florie's sporty Audi TT drew up at the security gate. Once parked she enjoyed the short walk in the crisp rising sun, now sitting low on the winter Gloucestershire horizon, to the main entrance where Florie was glad of the interior warmth of GCHQ.

On entering her section what attracted her attention was Jim Norris who was already sitting at his monitor,
"Oh my God Jim what time did you come in this morning?" she asked.
"Oh hi Florie. Well if the truth be known I never went home" he informed her in a low and slightly slurred voice.
"Why not Jim, today of all day's I want you to be fresh and on the ball."
"Don't worry Florie I am fully awake but I really was

expecting something to come through during the night and wanted to be the first to hear it ..but nothing, I was wrong."
Florie was a normal perceptive woman and realised that Jim had only stayed all night at his station as she turned him down for dinner the night before. He was sulking.
"I am going to make a coffee do you want one?" she asked him.
" No i'm fine I had one just a few minutes ago" he replied keeping his eyes averted from Miss D'Arcy.
Not wanting to risk any form of an atmosphere in the office on this the penultimate day she quietly made her way to her office and put on the coffee machine. Florie's first planned priority for the day was to call a group meeting and discuss any updates or ideas re: the attack which could possibly start within 24 hrs.
Then, just as she was taking the first sip of the full roasted, the phone rang,
"Hello D'Arcy here."
"Good Morning Florence, if I might call you that now we are acquainted, is this line still secure? the voice asked.
"Yes of course Jessica (MI6)"replied Florence.
"Oh good you recognised my voice. We have been chatting and come up with an idea. Did you manage to trace the mobile number of the 95.62hz transmission from Damascus?" Mrs Hardman asked.
"Give me a second and I will check" replied Miss D'Arcy and ran from the office to Dean's console where he was now munching into a ham sandwich.
"Dean did you manage to establish the mobile of the Damascus transmission?"
"Yes I think I did ..now let me see, oh yes here were are it's 0563 85436 but I think we missed out on the last digit" and proceeded to write the number down on a scrap piece of headed paper. Taking hold of the paper Florence ran back to her phone,

"Hello Jessica ..yes I have it, or rather most of it, here. It's 056385436 but the last digit is missing. Why do you want it?" Florence asked.
"Well we thought that our agent in Cairo who speaks fluent Egyptian could ring this number , obviously we will assume that it will be Zadran who answers, and pretend to be a member of the Egyptian Brotherhood who tells Zadran that the attack is to be cancelled. We will adapt the school reference coding in the hope he would believe the authenticity of the caller and cancel or at least postpone the attack. It could just unsettle him into making a mistake or some more phone calls which could enable us to trace the source of transmisson. We now have the NSA's satellite directly over Syria and with this number in it's memory banks will be able to place the location with only seconds of transmission."
"That sounds clever Jessica but how will you identify the last digit?"
"Don't worry about that our computers will sought that out. I will keep you informed, bye" and hung up.
With her receiver firmly replaced Miss D'Arcy made her way to the door and called Jim Norris into the office.
"Jim, just a development you should be aware of, I have just had MI6 on the phone and their Syrian agent is going to ring the Damascus mobile will have from the transcript and prompt a reaction so please advice your colleagues to report any echo's immediately. This could go either way. Sure you do not want a coffee?"

"No thanks Florie. This sounds interesting best get back to my console" replied Jim.

* * *

The soft traffic check points set up by a mixture of police and Territorial Army at Heathrow and now Gatwick,

Glasgow and Birmingham airports were beginning to cause traffic jams, not of a concerning length, but nevertheless of annoyance and concern to the passengers making their way to flights. No explanation, excepting that it was a traffic survey was offered to the general public. As the day progressed and the deadline became ever closer the comprehensiveness of the questioning and car searches increased and so did the reaction of the public. It would be around lunch time when the press were alerted to the overall situation and would begin to dispatch reporters and camermen to the various airports. They could only speculate as to what was going on as none of the services would release a word.

* * *

The minute Damian Arbuthnot heard Mrs Billgate-Hardman's ('B') voice on his phone a shiver ran down his Scottish back. Only when something difficult or dangerous comes up does his boss contact him personally. This was no exception.
"Hello Damian, I have a little task for your unique talent. I want you to utilise your spoken Egyptian like never before.." Mrs Hardman continued as she related the plan to her trusted special agent.
It took a while for the task to sink into Damian's head. At first it sounded reasonably straight forward but Damian realised the difficulty of trying to emulate a true Egyptian voice, which the recipient ought to be familiar with and he would not and should the deception fail what would the consequences be.
"Yes, 'B', I will try but you do realise the delicacy and complexity for me to pull off such a deception. One thing I could do is to have some Cairo noise in the background, say some singing prayers from a minaret., that might just

help convice Zadran of the reality of the call" Damian suggested.
"Good thinking Damian. You have just a few hours in which to prepare yourself as I want you to make the call at exactly 15:11hrs your time (13:11hrs UK time) then so that GCHQ will be ready to monitor any reply and we can trace the loction of the mobile should Zadran then use it."
"Ok 'B' leave it with me, goodbye."

* * *

It was now 10:30am in London as the PM called another meeting of COBRA for 11am, with the excepting of a GCHQ representative being present, as he wanted all the relevant members to the fully aquainted with the latest appraisal of the situation.
Big Ben could clearly be heard striking eleven as the various officials took their places around the oval table in the Cabinet room of 10 Downing Street.
The PM, Denis Morrison, called the meeting to order,
"Ladies and Gentlemen we have less than 24hrs before the proposed cyber attack might take place. Could you please update the committee as to your position thus far ... Fiona (Home Secretary) *can we start with you please"* the PM directed.
"Yes, good morning. At this time we have check points set up at strategic locations at Heathrow, Birmingham, Gatwick and Glasgow airports. So far nothing suspicious or out of the ordinary has been found. There has arisen a great deal of frustration from the public who have been told nothing. The press , as I am sure that you are aware, are proposing all soughts of hypotheses as to what is going on but none have guessed correctly ....yet! All international airlines have stepped up their security procedures at check-in and internal airport x-ray operators have been told to concentrate on electronic

devices."
"Ok how about you Jessica (MI6)?" asked the PM.
The rather arrogant head of MI6 took a gentle cough,
"Good morning. We are attempting to put a spanner in the works for Zadan, if it is he that is behind the attack, by placing a fake cancellation order to him on his mobile. It might work but what have we too lose at this stage as we have no other intel except to say that Zadran has been confirmed in Damascus"
"Thank you 'B' ".
It was now the turn for the portly Geoffrey Hallsworthy from MI5 (Internal Security) to update the committee,
"Not a lot to report I'm afraid, Fiona has covered most of it suffice to say we have picked up a great deal of chatter on 'Twitter' but it's all useless chit chat. Nothing of interest. We have 'picked up' several known Islamic targets and kept them , shall we say occupied, for the time being. That's it" quoted Mr Hallsworthy as he reached into his pocket for his pipe.
"Hum! Hum! " coughed Mrs Hardman *"No smoking in here Geoffrey!!"*
Before finally closing his official file Mr Morrison (PM) took to his feet and issued a statement,
"Very well I see we can do no more at this stage, however Fiona (Home Secretary) *give orders for the '999' services to be on full standby for tomorrow just in case the incident proves real and effective.* ***Tomorrow*** *is the 28th so let's all be alert. That's all"* and again vacated the Cabinet Room.

* * *

The two Al-Mawla agents were so relieved to pass through the security barrier at Brussels Centrale train station and get a view of the streamline Eurostar high speed train that

was soon to transport them into the heart of London at one hundred and eighty miles per hour. It signified to them that they had made it safely to London. On checking the departures board it showed they should arrive at
St Pancras at 1535hrs. Today was the 27th!
Their journey from Damascus had been long, arduous and not without stress, especially when clearing security at Sofia Airport (Bulgaria) and Brussels Airport where their Egyptian passports caused a few questions from the acute passport control security officer in Sofia who demanded an explanation of their reason for travelling to Brussels. The memorised story of visiting a sick friend in a little know Belgium village was convincing enough for them to gain entry aboard the Bulgaria Air flight but then later upon encountering the Belgium immigration control. There, the questioning was more intense, however by sticking to the same story and Zadran having the foresight to have obtained the correct tourist visas and bought return flight tickets to Sofia for four days later, also convinced the suspicious officer that he had no reason to detain them.
The TGV trainset of Eurostar was a new experience for the two Egyptians and when settled into the maximum cruising speed of just under two hundred miles per hour, they were agog with awe. It then took only an hour before the country view through the window was suddenly replaced with a dark blackness. They had entered the Channel Tunnel. As daylight re-emerged the two agents had made it to British soil which brought a satisfiying grin to both their tanned, beared faces.

The sight of the lush green countryside of rural Kent covered in a misty damp cloud seemed a strange environment for them to behold, afterall it was not quite the same as their homeland of dust, sand and, when in Damascus , a war torn zone of exploding shells. They both inwardly felt a tinged jealousy and a wanting of the peace

and tranquility of this strange land but the more implanted ideology of their fundalmental Islamic teachings would not allow them to ever partake. They may think and dream but they may not act. At this point the elder of the agents caressed his pocket Qur'an for extra comfort.
As the Eurostar drew to a halt in the beautifully renovated St Pancras station the agents had then to consult and master the confusing London Underground map for the journey they now decided to make direct to Hatton Cross , this being the closest tube station to the perimeter of Heathrow Airport, on the Victoria line to Green Park then changing to the Piccadilly line to Hatton Cross. With their limited supply of tattered and torn sterling currency Farook bought the tickets and muttered,
"The cost for such a short distance, they must be very rich here!"
This section of their journey they found to be the most difficult to navigate and together with the sheer quantity of people electing to travel underground just confirmed their distaste of the lifestyle of western living. Having narrowly avoided catching the wrong tube train to Uxbridge they successfully boarded the correct one for Heathrow.

The board for Hatton Cross was clearly visible through the tube window as the two entrepid Egyptians alighted to the platform whilst they searched for the way out.
Their lungfull of really **fresh** damp air, the first since entering the airport in Sofia , was uplifting to both their spirits so much so that they just stood in the station entrance for a couple of minutes to taste the decadent western oxygen before the younger of the duo decided to disappear and look for a public toilet.
As he disappeared out of sight back into the confines of the tube station the remaining Egyptian suddenly found himself being the centre of attention. Whilst standing on his own the beared , tanned young man wearing his

somewhat out of the ordinary attire caught the attention of one of the alert policemen assigned to the check point located just outside the tube station entrance ,
"Excuse me sir would you mind just coming over here please" the policeman requested in his normal polite manner. Farook, being the only one of the two who could understand english to any reasonable degree, was frozen to the spot with total surprise and amazement and did nothing.
"Sir would you come over here please" the policeman repeated in a somewhat more authoritative voice. Arising to his situation Farook saw no choice than to obey the request and slowly walking the few feet to the group of three policemen so innocently standing by their BMW cars.
" Are you English?" the policeman asked.
"Er no sir I am Egyptian from Egypt sir. I am here to see a friend" answered Farook in an obviously nervous voice.
"I need to have a look in your backpack please sir" the policeman continued and before Farook could object the bag had been removed from his back by one of the other policemen and placed on the roof of one of the BMW's. It did not take long to find the videocamera and mobile phone.

Meanwhile Farook's colleague, Mohammed, had just re-emerged from the station entrance only to see Farook being searched by the policemen. This sent shivers down his back and with an immediate instinct walked back into the station and covertly observed the proceedings from the safety of some cover offered by a newspaper stand.
"Where does your friend live sir" the first policeman then asked.
"Er Er London sir" replied Farook.
"Where in London? It's a big place you know."
Farook was caught on the spot so in his nervous dispossession quoted the first name that entered his head,

"Putney sir."
"So why are you here at Hatton Cross then sir?"
Now Farook was really struggling to continue his fictious story but manged to utter a few words,
"Er er is this not Putney sir?"
This reply only served to confirm the policeman's original suspicion leading him to say,
"Would you mind coming with us to the police station so we can have a few more words with you" grabbing Farook's arm and bungling him into the rear of one of the BMW's.
Mohammed, having clearly seen all that had happened quickly took advantage of the disappearance of two of the police cars and calmly walked to the side of the station entrance into the car park. He managed to avoid the check point but was now on his own. He could have no contact with Farook from now on in case the police might trace his mobile. From the company of his friend for the last few days .... he now felt so alone.
Within a few minutes , after taking the opportunity to sit on the grass with his eyes closed, Mohammed felt more composed and was even more determined to focus on his mission.
The solitude of the moment was suddenly broken by a an escalating voluminous Whoooooosh and upon looking up Mohammed saw a large airliner pass directly overhead barely ten metres above him. Standing up he observed that he was right at the landing end of one of Heathrow's runways. How convenient he thought to himself. His task was to report to Damascus the arrival of the British Airways A380 from New York in the morning and then film the impending crash. The position he was now located at was too close to the runway to be able to identity the Airbus in time to advise Zadran. Using his instinct he therefore began walking away from the airport, across the

main A30 highway and down Fagg's Road for some one hundred metres before turning left into Causeway. The flights were screaming in to land above his head every ninety seconds or so. Some two hundred metres along Causeway Mohammed came across a grass bank which sided a small reservoir. This could be a good vantage point, quiet, disceet and no police. Taking up a position on the bank Mohammed withdrew the small pair of binoculars from his backpack and began observing the incoming aircraft. The first he saw was the Emirates Boeing 777 which Mohammed estimated to be around a kilometre from touchdown. He could read the airline name and logo painted down the fuselage of the plane clearly and further timed it to be seventy five seconds from his confirmation of aircraft type to it's landing .. enough time to advise Zadran. So, assumimg that the aircraft would use the same runway the following morning Mohammed was confident that he had found a good spot for his dirty deed. It was now time to find somewhere to stay for the night and get some food as his stomach was beginning to rumble. His thoughts and concerns about his friend Farook must be put to the back of his mind and concentrate on the mission.
"This way sir" the policeman directed as he led Farook into the interview room. The short distance from the tube station to Heathrow's own police station on the other side of the airport took only eleven minutes.
With the nervous Egyptian sat at the barren table in walked a plain clothed gentleman in the forties who sat down on the opposite side to Farook.
"Well now, I see from your passport that you are Farook Sawalha. Is that correct?"
"Yes sir but why am I here?" Farook replied.
"Why did you come to UK via Sofia and Brussels and not direct from Egypt? the man asked.
There was a long pause as Farook did not have an answer that immediately came to hand then out of panic said,

"Er, er, er can I have a lawyer as I want to claim Political Asylam" Farook replied.
The man stood up,
"No chance. I have to advise you that I am from UK internal security (MI5) and am not satisfied with your situation. You will be held for further questioning" and off the man went to contact Mr Kevin McCloud at HQ.
The minutes passed as Farook sat in the cell contemplating the hopeless position he now found himself in.
His conclusion and final action was now inevitable. He carefully tore open the left lapel of his jacket, withdrew the pill stored inside and swallowed it. His final prayer to Allah was never completed before he fell to the ground.
It was not until 1824hrs (6:24pm) until the duty officer opened the cell door to check on the prisoner that the body was found laid out flat on the floor. The duty doctor was speedily called for who then officially pronounced the Egyptian was dead.

Kevin McCloud was furious when he was told at 1842hrs (6:42pm) as this fully confirmed that their one real chance of establishing some more information about the attack in just a few hours ...had gone. It also confirmed that the attack planned for the following day .... was real!
The Home Secretary went puce in the face with anger when she was informed and immediately requested an inquiry into the police procedures.
In their defence the Heathrow police station duty officer had ordered a thorough investigation of the clothes and effects of the dead Egyptian in the hope of uncovering some clues that might prove useful. It was the mobile phone which he rapidly arranged to have transported, by motorcycle with escort, to the SIS building on the River Thames in central London, this being the headquarters of MI5 and MI6.

Both Kevin McCloud and Jessica Hardman anxiously awaited the arrival of the phone and in the meantime had alerted the technical branch to standby.

* * *

It was exactly 15:11 hrs in Cairo as the afternoon **Asir** prayers began to be sung all over the city from the many Minerets. Damian stood near the window and lifted the phone to his ear,
"Salaam."
"Salaam, is that you Zadran?" Damian asked in his best Egyptian.
"Who is this?" Zadran asked.
"I am Riad from the Brotherhood and have been instructed to tell you that the School has been closed and the pupils are to go home."
"Who is this?" Zadran again asked with surprise and caution in his response.
Trying to maintain an open line for as long as possible knowing that GCHQ were listening in and for Zadran to hear the singing, Damian again resumed his Egyptian rhetoric,
"I repeat the School has been closed and the pupils are to go home. Do you understand Zadran?"
The line went silent for a few seconds as Zadran was not convinced of the authenticity of the call, then spoke,
"I do not know who you are" a few seconds of a further silence passed *"**Pray hard!**"* and switched of his mobile.
Damian with his usual aggresive but contained behaviour depressed his off button and returned to his coffee!

"Did you get a trace on that echo ?" Mrs Hardman asked the NSA operator who was on the telephone to her from Fort Mead, Maryland, USA.

Officer Dillon of SID (Signals Intelligence Directorate) was positive with his responce,
"Yes Ma'am. Source is 33 degrees 31 minutes 10 seconds N and 36 degrees 18 minutes and 12 seconds E."
"Excellent then send in a cruise missile onto those co-ordinates immediately!" ordered Mrs Hardman.
In the interests of time Officer Dillon had been given the authority to contact the modern destroyer USS Bainbridge, currently cruising in the eastern Mediterranean and give them the co-ordinates and authority to fire a cruise missile at that target. Without any undue delay Dillon signalled, via the satallite up-link, the code to fire to the Captain of Bainbridge who then relayed the order to his firing Officer.
The ship vibrated as the cruise missile departed it's launch tube and headed on it's pre-planned low trajectory towards Syria at four hundred kts.

Having smelt a rat with the telephone call Zadran decided to err on the side of caution and return to his basement HQ so paid for his coffee, ran from the cafe and started off down the road to his basement some four hundred metres west of the cafe.
Covering the sea at a height of two hundred feet and nine miles a minute the Tomahawk cruise missile soon crossed into Syrian territory and entered the area of Damascus.
The co-ordinates of the cafe, set into the inertial navigation system, directed the missile precisely into the roof exploding with an enormous bang sending debris over a wide area. The blast wave caught the back of Zadran sending him face down onto the road surface.
Slowly but surely he managed to raise himself to an upright position once again and timidly limped the remaining distance to his basement. If the missile had struck just ten seconds earlier then he would surely have been killed!
Knowing now for certain that someone was aware of his

planned attack tomorrow morning changed nothing for Zadran as his confidence in Asphan's ability to hack into the British computer system was high. With this obvious attempt upon his life he was more than ever determined to strike a blow at the decadent west.
"Ma'am we have a successful strike on the target. Images confirm target destroyed" Officer Dillon confirmed to Mrs Hardman.
"Good. Thank your organisation for their co-operation" she replied and removed her headsets.
Turning to Kevin,
"Let's just pray that Zadran was still in the building Kevin and this nightmare will now be over."
"By this time tomorrow we will know for sure Jessica" he replied.
"Possibly but let's not loose our vigilance yet. I suggest we keep this result under our hat for the time being which will still keep everyone focussed but we still require the result of the search from the mobile taken from the Heathrow suspect just in case" she suggested.
"I agree" was McCloud's reply.

Coincidentally it was only a few minutes before the transcript of the last few calls made from Farook's phone were presented on Jessica's desk.
On Mrs Hardman's close inspection most of the numbers turned out to be of little interest however there was one received from Zadran's mobile on the 26th, yesterday!
"How the hell did GCHQ miss that transmission? That could have been the vital one!!" she asked Kevin.
"God knows. Should I contact Miss D'Arcy and tell her?" he suggested.
"Yes better do that. Maybe it might sharpen them up!" she commented.

The **"European Photo-Book"** collection

Chapter Six

The 28th !! A Day never to be forgotten

As dawn broke the weather at London's Heathrow Airport was overcast supporting a light drizzle and with a wind of a constant ten kts blowing from 290 degrees so the decision of the airport manager was to use runway 27L for landing aircraft and 27R for take-off aircraft. Without realising it the implications of this decision may well prove to be disastrous as this meant that all landing aircraft would indeed be coming into land over Hatton Cross tube station as per the previous day.
Aboard the new British Airways A380, Flt BA 2534, inbound from New York the flight deck crew Captain Newman, a very senior and experienced pilot having served with British Airways for nearly fifteen years and recently converted to this brand spanking new A380 Super Jumbo from the ageing Boeing 747-400 and Senior First Officer Bashir, who had joined British Airways from Iberia Airlines some three years pevious having been in a similar post on Airbus 340's, started to prepare for the landing phase of their long eight and a half hour flight from JFK airport in the United States.
Currently at ten thousand feet on a heading of 090 degrees the A380 was homing in on the Biggin beacon from whence they would initiate a long rate 1 turn left onto an approximate heading of 270 degrees to pick up the ILS (Instrument Landing System) for a three degree glideslope approach to runway 27L at Heathow Airport.
"Arrival checks please Mr Bashir" Captain Newman requested which, having referred to the flight manual, he successfully completed.
Newman then made his arrival call,
"Heathrow TCA (Terminal Control Centre) this is G-ASAC. Flt No. BA 2534 inbound from New York at flight level 10 approaching Biggin at 10 minutes."
The TCA radar approach at Swanwick replied,
"BA 2534 I have you on scope continue on your present

heading. Advise over Biggin."
" BA 2534 will do."
Newman then turned towards his co-pilot,
"Advise cabin crew for landing please."
"Very well sir ...Cabin crew prepare for landing" which resonated throughout the gigantic body of the A380 from the overhead speakers on all three decks.
No doubt all of the four hundred and fifty nine passengers and twenty five crew were glad to hear the announcement as the Atlantic crossing had not been the smoothest albeit that this was the inaugural flight of this newly purchased half billion pound giant of the skies.

* * *

Mohammed wasted no time when he awoke to find the hostel bedside clock read 0630hrs (6:30am). There was no time to wash, eat or pray. The target aircraft was due around 0735hrs (07:35am) and he had a twenty five minute walk to his selected observation point from the "Green Man Hostel" .
With the Camcorder, binoculars and mobile (fully charged) safely stowed in his coat pockets he made his way downstairs and out into the damp dark morning. The winter sun, what little was visible, was breaking the horizon casting it's rays of daylight across the sordid landscape of West Hounslow. Mohammed headed west down the Great West Road towards the airport. The placitude of the walk allowed him thoughts of what might have become of his friend Farook. Visions of him languishing in a police cell concentrated his mind. The reality of him being dead was not accepted.
However the constant roar of jet engines above him kept interrupting his thoughts as one by one the early morning arrivals of the long haul flights completed their final

approach to runway 27L but assurredly confirmed that the aircraft were using the runway over his observation point.
It was just mindboggling to Mohammed, the simple Egyptian from Memphis (ancient capital of Egypt sited on the outer fringes of Cairo) as to just how many aircraft, all full with people, came to London. One every ninety seconds he counted.

* * *

The PM had re-convened COBRA for 0800hrs (8:00 am) gathering all the authorities together for a more rapid and decisive response should anything actually happen during the course of the day.
Miss D'Arcy and her team were all at their stations at GCHQ in preparation for any echoes, by 0630hr (06:30am)
The police and Army checkpoints at all four airports were trying hard to question people without causing too much disruption to the thousands of passengers making their way to the check-in's.
The airport emergency services were on full alert at all four airports.

What more could be done? It was the 28th

* * *

Asphan, the young Yemeni had successfully negotiated his way through the ashen pink morning light ..it was going to be a bright and sunny day in Damascus, to the street where Zadran was anixiously waiting in the basement. It was 0810hrs (08:10 am Damascus which was 06:10hrs in

London). One hour twenty five minutes to go before initiating the cyber command programme.

Tripping over a few bricks as he entered the house, Asphan called out at the top of the long stairs leading to the basement,

"Abasin are you there?"

"Salaam yes of course I am here. Is that you Asphan?"

"Yes."

Zadran was nervous that his friend had been a little late but now calmed down as everything was present for the attack to be now carried out.

"Abasin I will have to quickly change the laptop processor for this one. Please get me a strong light so that I can see the screwheads" Asphan requested as he turned over the computer to access the sealed door underneath.

"Why Asphan?"

"Because the Sony icore5 will not be fast enough. It will only take me a couple of minutes. Don't worry we have plenty of time" he stated.

Sure enough it took exactly four minutes to complete the change,

"Here Abasin connect in this broadband cable whilst I connect to other end into the landline network" Asphan commented as he searched around to find the connecting landline telephone plate. Time to activate the Sony . It opened up perfectly with it's normal ding-dong theme.

"I think I will just open a few websites to check the new speed and double check that all is working properly" advised Asphan.

"Excellent we are ready to go Abasin."

* * *

"Heathrow TCA this is BA 2534. Above Biggin" reported Captain Newman.
"BA 2534 you are clear to turn to 276 degrees and descend to 5000 feet" replied the TCA controller.
"Engage ILS on 109.5 please Mr Bashir" Newman ordered.
"ILS code identified and selected sir."
As the captain eased his tiny joystick right to level the A380 on a heading of 276 degrees, allowing for the small crosswind, the vertical and horizontal needles of the Omni bearing indicator clearly indicated that the aircraft was correctly established on the three degree glideslope for his landing on runway 27L.

* * *

"I have logged onto the British NATS (National Air Traffic System) *Abasin, what is the time?"* asked Asphan
" It's precisely 09:05 am (07:05am London) *Asphan"* advised Zadran.
"Very well time to engage the Heathrow ILS computers using the rather tenuous link from NATS and open my corrupting programme and wait for the sighting from your agents before engaging" he spoke out loudly.
"*Very well. Where are they?. Where are they ?"* Zadran kept on repeating under his breathe, *"Where are they?"*
With only a few minutes to go before the target would be expected to be within his colleagues vision Zadran was building a small band of sweat across his brow.

* * *

Mohammed had by now firmly established himself on the grassy bank by the reservoir that he found the previous day and was scouring the lightening sky on the runway approach for his target ...

..the British Airways A380.

As he rotated the thumbscrew of his binoculars a Swiss A340 gradually focussed in view. He could easily read the airline name so felt confident in his ability to identify the British Airways jet when it appeared. The third aircraft that appeared was a British Airways aircraft ... but was it the A380? Having been supplied with a picture of the 380 Mohammed, a little confused with the head on view, concluded the it was not. He was right it was a Boeing 747-400!
His watch indicated 0715hrs (07:15am), time to contact Zadran he concluded and proceeded to dial in the numbers (963) 056385436..2
"*Salaam*" the voice echoed.
"*Is that you Abasin? It's Mohammed.*"
"*Ah at last Mohammed is everything ok. Are you at Heathrow airport?*" Zadran asked with undue care as he realised that it would now be too late for any listeners to act and change anything at this stage.
"*Farook has been taken by the police but I am in position and waiting for the aircraft*" advised Mohammed.
"*Good keep the line open from now on*" ordered Zadran.

* * *

It was with a loud shout of excitement that Dean called out," *He's back, he's back!*" as the whole of the middle east section of GCHQ suddenly burst into life.
"*Quickly give me a transcript*" shouted Miss D'Arcy in an excited state.
"*It's a two way conversation with a man called Mohammed and fuck! he's at Heathrow*" shouted Dean.

Without any delay Florence lifted the receiver and speed-dialled Jessica at MI6,
"Jessica, the target is Heathrow. We have just this second picked up a conversation between Zadran and his contact called Mohammed who is at Heathrow now!"
"Ok Florence leave that with me. Get onto NSA for a possible fix of the agent at Heathrow and let me know, bye."
By the time Miss D'Arcy got through to Officer Dillon at Fort Mead, the on-the-ball decorated agent had already established a fix on Mohammed's mobile,*"It's around 400 yards from the end of runway 27L. That's the best I can do for you"* he confirmed.
In her haste to now contact Jessica she forgot to sign off with Dillon having depressed the phone cut-off button and speed- dialled MI6 once again.

* * *

"BA 2534 continue your approach, for runway 27L, wind 290 @ 9 kts contact approach on 117.725. Good day sir" was the final instruction from the TCA controller.*"Good day"* repeated the Airbus captain.
Beep, beep accompanied by a flashing bulb, was clearly audible in the A380 cockpit as it passed over the outer marker located exactly seven point two miles from the threshold of 27L,
"Lower gear and select thirty degrees of flap please Mr Bashir" ordered Captain Newman who then proceeded to contact Heathrow Approach.
"Heathrow Approach this is BA 2534 inbound from New York on final approach 27L."
"Good morning sir. Continue your descent on ILS. Wind 290 degrees 10 kts" replied the female controller with a

sexy but sharply clear voice.
Beep, beep again was heard indicating the aircraft was directly overhead the middle marker at 3500 feet from the threshold!

* * *

"I have it Abasin I have it in sight" shouted Mohammed into his mobile.
"Now Asphan now now!" Ordered the excited Zadran. Immediately Asphan drew his full focus to his specially written programme. Typing in the code DFRTER: the laptop screen changed to a series of technical graphs and figures confirming to Asphan that his progamme was fully engaged: he depressed the enter key and off went the cyber signal at the speed of light, down the broadband cable, off to the transmitter, up to the satellite link then back down to the receiver at Swanwick and into the ILS computer at Heathrow. Now came the clever bit, which was why Asphan was selected for this mission, the cyber signal attached itself to the carrier wave of the 90 hz ILS signal which relayed the correct glideslope to the landing aircraft thus entering the main flying computer within the British Airways A380. The cyber signal contained the order for the A380 autopilot to engage and falsely identify that the aircraft was three hundred feet too high for the approach therefore would close the throttles of the four huge Rolls Royce Trent engines and lower the nose to re-establish the correct glidepath as it knew it! This it did.
Immediately the speed and height alarms burst into life as the joystick was pulled forward from the captain's left hand,
"Fucking hell!! what's happening!!" Newman screamed out as the aircraft began to loose height.
"The auto has engaged sir!" shouted Bashir.
"Then cancel it NOW!!!!"

"It won't respond. It won't respond. I cannot cancel!"

"I have no control, no control!" cried Newman as he saw the houses of Hounslow rapidly approaching.
"Mayday, Mayday BA 2 ...." was all that Captain Newman could transmit before the enormous aircraft plunged nose first into the terraced houses of Cavalry Crescent in a huge impact before some of the remaining fuel spewed out from the ruptured wing tanks and ignited into a huge explosion resulting in a red/black cloud of smoke emerging high into the sky from the Crescent.
"It worked Abasin it's down! A massive ball of fire" Mohammed joyfully screamed into the mobile phone.
"Calm down Mohammed calm down can you see the next aircraft coming into land?" Zadran hurriedly asked.
Raising the binoculars once again,
"Yes."
"What airline is it?"
"It's , it's erm American . It's got American written on it " advised Mohammed, *"but it's climbing ."*
Patting Asphan on the back Zadran, in a very soft voice this time, said,
"Go my friend send the signal again. Let's see if we can get two for the price of one!"
"Very well if you are sure. Let's hope it's still captured on the ILS wave" replied the Egyptian.

"What the hell! She's engaged auto, disconnect the auto Bob" shouted the American captain.
"Won't disengage Skipper, won't disengage" the First Officer declared as the nose began the drop as the engine revolutions fell to 50 percent power,

"Mayday this is AA4539 auto jammed. Taken control. No power. We are going in. W........"
It would be no more than one hundred metres from the burning wreckage of the A380 that the American
Boeing 777 would strike the ground in Beavers Lane. Once again the detached houses this time , their occupants and the people on board the aircraft got burnt to death in the resulting fireball.
In his binoculars the duty controller in Heathrow's control tower clearly saw the burning hulks and immediately ordered all incoming flights to abort their approaches with the utmost haste and fly north for a diversionary landing at Stansted and Luton. He also ordered an immediate ban on any aircraft movements on the ground. The airport gradually came to a standstill.
The eight police cars with full blue roof and grill lights flashing and sirens screaming, sped to the eastern end of the airport via the Eastern Perimeter Road and onto the Great West Road, joining the multitude of airport fire engines and Land Rovers, before turning into Green Lane towards the two huge vertical columns of black smoke.
However it was the astute driver of car 'Bravo 89' that decided to continue on down Fagg's Road and into the Causeway towards the reservoir when he observed a single figure walking towards the crash site carrying a videocamera to his eye. Drawing up alongside the lonesome figure he constable lowered his passenger window and spoke to the surprised man,
"Excuse me sir what are you filming?"
With images of his friend Farook being escorted away by police the previous day still fresh in his mind, Mohammed now himself being confronted by the same uniform, panicked and took flight down the road as fast as he could. Putting his foot hard down on the accelerator the constable proceeded after the assailant in a cloud of tyre smoke but

as he overtook and braked and before jumping out of the car the suspect had jumped over a wooded fence and was fleeing up the bank of the reservoir. The rather portly constable however could not make it over the fence which left him with little alternative that to draw his pistol from it's holster and shout with the full volume of his voice,
"Stop, stop or I will shoot!"
In normal circumstances the police in UK are not armed, except for those on airport duties who are cleared for sidearms and machine guns and together with the hightened security status now pending at all four major UK airports, the constable had the right to shoot.
Whether or not he heard the order or just decided to ignore it whilst about to reach the apex of the slope, the suspect did not stop. Again the constable shouted the order but with no response from the suspect.
Bang! as the first shot rang out, then another bang as the second shot brought the suspect to the ground who then unceremoniously rolled down the slope coming to a halt at the wooded fence. At this point having received a distress call from his colleague, Panda car 'Sierra 37' drew up in front of 'Bravo 89' with it's two occupants leaping out to assist the constable who by this time was leaning over the fence with his revolver pointing at the motionless suspect.
Immediately the two police officers pulled the fence down to reveal the tanned skinned suspect lying unconscious with blood pouring from the bullet wound in his lower back.

It was Mohammed!

An ambulance was called for whilst all three policemen searched the body and nearby grass bank for identification and possible weapons. All they found was the passport, camcorder, mobile phone and a few crumpled up notes of money.

* * *

Being remote from the carnage at Heathrow in her ivory tower at Bankside in central London Mrs Billgate-Hardman was able to think straight and relatively unpressurised so retained the presence of mind to re-contact Officer Dillon at Fort Mead to check if the NSA had traced the source of the transmission that was talking to the suspect at Heathrow a few seconds earlier which served to confirm that Zadran had not be killed in the earlier cruise missile strike ..by God they had.
"Yes Ma'am. It originated from a street in the north-east not far from the last target" he advised.
"Brilliant then can you send another missile to those co-ordinates ASAP!" Ms Hardman requested.
"Very well Ma'am consider it done" as he rapidly contacted the Captain of USS Bainbridge for the second time.
In the absence of Presidential orders for a second firing, but fully informed of the terrorist attack on London especially as an American plane had been downed, the Captain nervously agreed to the launch , so ordered the firing of a second Tomahawk cruise missile to take out the target at the co-ordinates provided by Dillon.
For the second time in the space of twenty four hours an American missile sped from the deep blue waters of the Mediterranean Sea deep into Syrian territory at tree top height. The few minutes of flight soon passed before the one thousand four hundred kilogram missile with it's four hundred and fifty kilogram warhead of high explosive ploughed into it's target causing a mighty explosion, amongst the many from Assad's continual assault, bringing the six houses crashing down in a cloud of compacted dust that radiated outwards from the centre of the explosion at high speed.
Eventually the heavier dust settled to reveal that most of

the street had simply disappeared into a pile of rubble with the occasional fire smoking away.
The scene fell eerily silent.... until the sound of a few bricks being moved could be just heard from the basement of
No.8. Wounded, but not fatally, by falling debris and covered in a thick layer of dust and sand the unbelievably lucky Abasin Zadran had managed to evade death for the second time within the last day. Carefully he pushed varying amounts of debris aside and managed to crawl up the long stairs dragging his crushed legs until he entered the morning daylight and some fresher air which would help curtail his coughing. There were no upper floors of his house left save part of the rear dining room wall which stood aloof like a monument.
As he crawled into what was once the street Zadran unknowingly grabbed hold of a single shoe, which he immediately recognised as that belonging to his friend Asphan. The left foot was still within the trainer but unattached from the leg. Zadran assumed that his Egyptian genius had perished.
He lay there alone, in the street, gazing up into the pale blue sky trying to work out what had happened. Could it have been a stray rocket from Assad's army ..maybe, but then being involved in two near misses in such a short time had to be more than a coincidence ..he had to have been the target. Then he remembered the hoax call from Cairo .. of course that was to trace his mobile transmission, but by whom? he thought to himself as he lay there bleeding profusely from his crushed and obviously broken right leg.

* * *

When Florence D'Arcy was informed of the tragic unfolding of the events at Heathrow her first reaction, apart from burying her head in her cupped hands, was one of totaly bewilderment as to how the attack was performed.

She new it would be from a cyber source but how technically were the two aircraft brought down? On consulting with her whole distraught section none could offer an explanation. All Dean could suggest was to be able to listen to the cockpit voice recorder which might well offer some clues.

* * *

Both crash scenes were one's of utter devastation, carnage and activity as dozens of fire engines, ambulances and police cars, from all the local stations of Hounslow, Isleworth, neighbouring Osterley and even as far afield as Twickenham were doing their utmost to qwell the flames with Co2 and water whilst attempting to enter the broken aircraft bodies to search for possible suvivors.
The consequence of a crash at so low an altitude was that all the passengers would have been still inside following the impact. It was a strange sight to see the mighty prestigious Airbus A380 almost in tact. Apart from the nose being severely crushed, the fuselage, wings and tail sat there at an angle of around sixty degrees. The freshly painted white body was now blackened and charred from the intense heat except for the eighty foot tailplane which stood majestically unscathed proudly showing it's red, white and blue Ensign logo to the world. Both wings had detached themselves from the mainframe but still more or less in the correct alignment. The strangest thing of all was that the enormous outermost Trent 900 engine on the starboard wing was still rotating on idle power, no doubt feeding from residue fuel in the tank and engine reservoir.Above the general demure din a loud voice could be heard coming from the tail of the Airbus,
"I've found one, I've found one alive here in the rear section!" the fireman screamed from the rear port exit door.

"Get a ladder and stretcher up there fast" ordered the Hounslow fire Chief and with total professional haste one of his firetrucks backed up to the aircraft and raised it's ladder to full extension. Even before the ladder has completed it's travel three burly firemen were fully prepared at the top and lept into the open but slanted doorway. The sight that beheld them was nothing like what they had seen before: hundreds of charred bodies sitting securely strapped in their seats but facing downwards towards the ground excluding three of the female cabin crew whose intensely frightened stare unsettled them as they had occupied the rear facing crew seats."Down here,down here" directed the fireman.
Working their way down the inclined walkway with the stretcher in tow the three men were greeted with the sight of, what was a beautiful young lady in her twenties dressed in a short skirt and v-necked jumper sitting slumped in the outside aisle seat. The flames had engulfed her like the rest of the passengers but somehow she was clinging onto life. The severity of the burns was all too obvious to the four firemen to the extent that the leading fireman questioned her rescue. What sort of a life would she now have he asked himself. Maybe they should just let her go peacefully. The sudden silence that befell confirmed to the Chief that all four were of a similar mind. However given those few seconds of serious thought was enough to convince him that it was not his or his colleague's decision to make. The rescue would continue so with extreme consideration he attached the oxygen mask over the poor girl's face trying hard not to endear any further pain.

The action to then get her onto the inclined stretcher took the guile, ingenuity and strength of all four but eventually they succeeded. Having securely strapped the patient down the chief then radioed for the winch to very gingerly take up the slack and gently, so very gently to ease the stretcher up to the rear doorway from where it could be lowered to the ground. Once the poor girl was in the ambulance rapidly making it's way to the specials burns unit of Charing Cross Hospital in Hammersmith with the help of a two car police escort, Dr. Robertson could carry out a good examination. The jolting and turning of the speeding vehicle did not help in his examination of the poor girl's body but nevertheless soon came to the conclusion that

never in his relatively short professional career had he seen such burns. How this desparately courageous young lady still clung onto life was a mystery to him. Her clothes had literally melted into the putrid skin which inturn was not always attached to anything but it was her eyes that severely affected him: they had melted away into ....enough! Dr. Robertson could not hold back any more and brought up his breakfast all over the vehicle floor.

Back at the second wreckage site the American 777-200 which had also departed from the United States, Chicago to be precise, had impacted the ground from a greater height and speed which resulted in a more savage but some would say a possibly more humane disaster as the deaths of all on board would have been virtually instantaneous. There were no survivors. Virtually nothing recognisable was left of the Boeing frame except for some tailfin skin painted in the new blue and red striped livery of American Airlines. The consequent fireball had been more intense than that the A380 cremating all two hundred and thirty nine passengers and crew.
It was a similar ordeal that befell the fire crews that attended the Airbus but on this occasion the bodies would require to be identified with reference to dental records and any surviving personal effects!
Soon the familiar site of white vans with satellite dishes atop pointing skywards appeared on the scene as the media

were anxious to transmit the story and live pictures of the smoldering wreckage around the world. First on the Airbus scene at Cavalry Crescent was the huge 'Sky ' TV team of four vehicles fronted by their well-known and compact figure of broadcaster Miss Stephanie Flowers, who was precariously perched on her stepping board, speaking to the world through her microphone. On the other side of the street busily setting up their equipment was the BBC, ITV and RT teams. Meanwhile at the Boeing site was another 'Sky' unit plus CNN and CBS alongside several digital channel teams.

Within minutes the whole world would be aware of the atrocious and cowardly act of terrorism that had taken place on the western fringes of London.... including Zadran and his compatriots in Tehran and Cairo.

The main priority of the Crash Investigation Unit of the CAA (Civil Aviation Authority) which duly arrived after about an hour following the first crash at the British Airways site, was the recovery of the 'Black Boxes ' (FDR Flight Data Recorders) of both aircraft to be taken away to the Farnborough Labs for immediate extensive analysis. Integral to the large oblong orange coloured unit (FDR) is a cockpit voice recorder on which is stored the conversations of the cockpit flight crew for the duration of the flight. As design would have it these FDR boxes are always located in the tail section of all aircraft, as this is deemed the area of least impact in the event of a crash, which was where the CIU headed for with the aid of several firemen to keep any flames at bay and to cool down the metalwork.

With all the emergency units at full stretch a tailback of many, many ambulances, at both sites, had built up into a river of white vehicles awaiting to take the hundreds of chared bodies in their individual body bags to a section of the main British Airways maintenance hanger on the south side of the airport, some half mile from the A380 site, which had rapidly been cleared of aircraft and vehicles to accommodate the bodies where a formal identification might be carried out in peace and quiet.

* * *

Back at the reservoir an ambulance has arrived to pick up Mohammed and to relieve the policemen to go and assist with the the now growing crowd of spectators. During a brief examination of his dying patient, who grabbed the doctor's arm, bowed over to hear the last few quietly spoken words,
"I go to heaven for my part in this. The brit............." and with an long slow exhalation of breathe Mohammed passed away to join his friend Farook.

* * *

An air of despondency fell heavily over GCHQ as the reality of the situation hit home. It was Jim , with the aid of his i-Pad4, who provided the up-to-date pictures of the carnage at Heathrow showing 'Sky TV's' Miss Flower's hard hitting and scathing attack on the authorities who, in her eyes, should have been able to prevent this atrocity,. Little did she know what had gone on beforehand. The whole team in Cheltenham took this attack personally and all to a man felt like going public to clear any suspicious fingers pointing at them, but being the 'quiet' agency that they are this could not happen!
Even during this depressing period most of the middle-east section were still listening out for echos from the middle-east that might have connections with Zadran or the attack on British Airways and American Airlines: but so far nothing. The airwaves had suddenly gone very quiet.

Miss D'Arcy kept in continual contact with both Jessica at MI6 HQ and The Home Secretary so that any leads or new information could be immediately exchanged between them.
Both 'Black Boxes' received instant attention upon their arrival at the Farnborough Accident Investigation Unit and due to their armoured protection were able to be transcribed very easily and without any delay. With the full report on his desk only some two hours after the arrival of the boxes on the base Professor Armstrong, the head of the investigation department, was able to confirm that both aircraft were on autopilot which had correctly identified the inaccurate settings of the ILS altitude. It was also firmly established beyond any doubt that both altitude readings suddenly changed just seconds before impact. So Professor Armstrong's simply arrived at final conclusion was that somehow both aircraft's autopilot computers had been compromised with an unauthorised command .. a cyber virus in other words and further, in his professional opinion, the only way that this signal could have entered the computers was through the ILS carrier wave. A very clever and well executed idea he thought to himself.
Once Mrs Billgate-Hardman ('B') was in possession of this knowledge she immediately advised Miss D'Arcy who in turn held a certain respect for this clever and daring idea.
Still the airwaves held their silence so confirmation of Zadran's death was not forthcoming despite several attempts by MI6 to establish contact with his mobile phone whose line was open but not being answered. Zadran had now become cautious with it's use.

* * *

Gathering all his weight onto his left leg whilst being

propped up by crutch of gash wood painfully resting under his right armpit Zadran limped down what remained of the street making his way home. Angered by the death of Asphan who had been his friend for so long and now fully realising that he was a target for the Americans decided that he would find his way to safety in Cairo and to disappear under the radar amongst known colleagues for at least the next six months, let the furor of world publicity die down as well as getting medical attention to his broken leg and other minor injuries. To this end he would make arrangements to be escorted to Beirut in Lebanon from where he could enlist the cooperation of friendly sympathisers to could covertly sail him along the Israeli and Sinai coasts to the Egyptian harbour of Port Fuad. From there he could easily and safely make his way onto Cairo to shelter under the safe and welcoming wing of the Eygptian Brotherhood.

The 28th closed but with a heavy heart in western Europe.

Would there be repercussions?

The **"European Photo-Book"** collection

Chapter Seven

The Aftermath

Two days passed before the official list of the seven hundred and twenty three passengers and crew plus the further sixty four residents of Cavalry Crescent and Beaver Lane who lost their lives in the two disasters was released: it included some rather important and influential personages.

American Airlines Flt AA 974

Robert McMurray ..Director of JP Morgan Chase Bank.

Dorothy Foster ..Director of JP Morgan Chase Bank.

British Airways Flt BA 2534

Rodrick Barnes ..Official (minor) in the British Government.
Edwina Stobbart ..Granddaughter of British Minister of Employment.
Dr.Ian Stewart ..Director of British Airways.

but the most evocative casualty, which did nothing to ease world tension especially in the middle-east theatre was, **Halim Pinhas** and his small negotiating team from the Syrian Government who were covertly travelling to London for exploratory talks with the Foreign Office having just completed preliminary discussions with the American Department of Foreign Affairs over a possible solution for the civil strife in Syria.
Nobody outside the closed network of the Government departments of the US, UK and Syria would have had knowledge of the team's presence on board the BA airliner

BA 2534:

or had there been a leak???

Maybe it was just an unfortunate coincidence ..only time and future investigations would reveal the truth.

With this knowledge having now having been revealed to MI6 and GCHQ the vigilant and intense watch on middle-east airwaves was to be continued into the near future in the hope that evidence of the negotiating team's murder had been planned and was the reason for the destruction of the aircraft at Heathrow. If no evidence was to be forthcoming within , say the next month or so, then MI6 and the Governments of Britain and America would have no option than to believe that British Airways and American Airlines were the targets all the time; in other words UK and US assets. Both aircraft clearly and proudly displayed their national representations on the body of the aircraft which to a terrorist would be considered to be a strike on that country.

That conclusion would most certainly lead to a more serious situation as both Governments would have a more public outcry for a military reprisal. Should British and American bombs followed by 'boots on the ground' knowingly to the world's public hit Syrian soil then a series of uncontrollable events, involving Iran and thier Hezbollah allies in Lebanon and Gaza plus Israel and even Russia, might well occur which could well lead to a third world conflict.

This could not be allowed to be contemplated so to that end both the American President O'Hara and British Prime Minister Denis Morrison agreed for it to be publicly known that the attack on the two aircraft at London's Heathrow Airport might have been solely to kill the Syrian team and that the terrorists could not be sure which of the two aircraft they were travelling on so took out both. This would by no means qwell the rising public anger in both countries but would nevertheless go some way to reduce the heat in the tension.

With Heathrow now having been closed for most of the 28th and MI6 along with the British Government convinced that the attack had been completed, the airport Directive decided on the re-opening of the northern runway 27R and allow take-offs and landings as the traffic chaos in UK airspace was considerable, to the point of becoming dangerous. It would not be to the following day that runway 27L was also once again open for normal operations.

With a round the clock recovery operation fully in place the removal of the aircraft wreckages was completed by the 1st of October at which point the houses that had been either destroyed or damaged were being re-built and as a gesture of goodwill both airlines agreed to pay several thousands of pounds in compensation to the families of the victims who lived in the Cavalry Crescent and Beavers Lane area afterall it was distinctly possible that they had all worked at Heathrow as ninety five percent of all the airport groundstaff lived within the Hounslow, Osterley, Feltham and Heston zones of west London.

Using reference to the flight manifests of BA2534 and AA974 plus international dental records (All of the relatives of the deceased were spared the grim ordeal of personal identification of the chared remains) all the bodies had their identity confirmed and were now, with the help of the Royal Air Force and United States Air Force, being released for the families to bury the remains at their requested destinations with dignity and grace.

Gradually but very gradually the operation of Heathrow Airport was beginning to get back to normal, however, not before the ILS computers were further safeguarded against any form of viral or cyber attacks.

Understandably there was no let up from the media whose speculation and vivid imagination served only to stir up hatred and resentment amongst the many anti-Islamic groups buried in the British and American populations. Several incidences of street violence broke out mainly in the north of England and the suburbs of Washington and Los Angeles. Local police tried their hardest to keep the factions apart but at times found that difficult to achieve. These groups wanted revenge, albeit that neither Government had ever issued any direct reference as to the actual culprits of the disaster.
These were tense times especially in the United States as memories of the twin towers disaster of 9/11 in New York bore heavily on the minds of so many. The people wanted answers and then action.

Two weeks of further tension passed with several discussions in the House of Commons and the Senate at which the opposition called for answers ...at this point there were none to give despite the pressure being brought to bear on MI6 and the NSA. Mrs Hardman (MI6) could not stand up in a court of Law and confirm to the world that the terrorist Abasin Zadran was behind this act of terrorism. She had no concrete proof. Yes she had her personal proof with the transmission transcripts but this would **not** be enough to possibly start a middle-east war in Syria if an open Government declaration was to be made against anti-Government Islamic factions in Damascus.
It just happened that an agreement over the future of chemical weapons in the region was reaching a positive platform and no-one, least of all the Americans wanted to jeopardize the delicate negotiations especially as the Russians were showing signs of a capitulation.
It was agreed with the sanctioning of both Governments

that MI6 and American Special Services that a joint maximum covert effort be put into operation within theatre in the middle-east. It was to be established beyond any doubt as to the final demise of Zadran and his colleagues enlisting the use of planted operatives from both organisations and if he was to be found alive he was to be taken , alive if possible and put on public trial or failing that to be executed and the body to be videoed for confirmation of death before disposal in the depths of the Mediterranean Sea.

The hunt began in earnest.

Political tensions were not just limited to western Europe and the States as events were coincidently turning nasty in Egypt as well but for a different reason. The Brotherhood's President Kalesh, who had been the resently and legally elected President of Egypt, had been upsetting a great deal of the population of the country with his introduction of strict Islamic ideals. In the modern 21st century many millions of Egyptians had departed from the old ways and encompassed the advantages of a Democratic way of living. Kalesh was determined to reverse this trend which had induced riots in the central area of Cairo. Kalesh either by ignorance or ill advice from his council paid no heed to this disturbance in his policy making.
He had badly mis-calculated as the riots, day by day grew and grew until the morning of the 30th of September when all hell broke loose in Tahrir Square with tear gas and violence requiring the Army to intervene to curb a full civil war from breaking out within Egypt. The death toll mounted as the Brotherhood supporters fought against the army who basically showed support for the
non-Brotherhood community. By the end of the next day the army had suffered enough casualties and desparately

wanted to enforce their authority on the situation and so arrested President Kalesh, putting him under house arrest until such time as a trial could be arranged. This had the effect of suppressing the uprising but drove the remaining illegal Brotherhood faction underground from where they would plan a comeback.

Zadran in his total ignorance of the changing circumstances in Cairo, eventually arrived in the city with two of his sympathisers and found his way to a safe house in yet another basement in a house in Farag Ln situated just north east of the central zone.

Now, being advised of the unpopularity of his Brotherhood comrades and the imprisonment of his friend Kalesh, Zadran felt that his first priority was to arrange for his leg to be attended to before getting involved in any action. The pain on the sea crossing from Beirut had become more intense and his concentration on important matters was waning.

The sympathetic doctor did a good job allowing Zadran to walk comfortably but still aided with a stick and with his limited mobility back decided to accept his invitation to visit the new secret underground headquarters of the Brotherhood movement located in Talaat Harb Str. in Cairo centre. The journey from Farag Ln took longer than usual as many check points had been established by the army which had to be circumvented by using tiny backstreet passages. Eventually the party of three arrived at the entrance to No. 32, which supported a tatty signboard for the 'King Tut Hostel' on the eighth floor, who then made their way up the concrete stairs to the second floor. Following a pre-determined knocking code on the front door of the office the party entered and were shown to one of the rooms where sat on an old barrel was the colourful character of Habibah, an old friend of of Zadran's from the past,

"*Tah'yati habibi* (Greetings my friend) *How are you? There has been a few changes since you left Abasin"* spoke the young Egyptian.

"Marhaba Hi. Habib. So I see. Did you hear of my success in Britain?" asked Zadran.
"So that was you?"
"Yes with a little help from Asphan Rachid" replied Zadran.
"Oh that geek. How is the boy?" asked Habibah.

"Dead."
"Oh no sorry to hear that. You know that Kalesh is under arrest and that Mohammed has taken over the leadership" Habibah went on to inform Zadran.
"Yes, when can I see Mohammed as I need to inform him of the details of UK" continued Zadran.
"Phone him now on this number and I'm sure he will be glad to hear your voice and could do with some good news!" Habibah advised handing him the piece of paper with Mohammed's private number written on it.
It was with slight intrepidation that Zadran removed his mobile from his pocket realising that it could have been this that had directed the American missiles to his locations in Damascus a couple of weeks ago but then, he thought, how could they do this in neutral Cairo so he felt safe in using it ...a bad mistake!
"Salaam Mohammed, it's Abasin."
"Aha Zadran, Salaam. Good to hear from you" replied Mohammed (Mr X).
Wishing to keep the transmission as short as possible as perhaps now he felt he was having second thoughts about being detected Zadran then went on to say,
"I am in Cairo. Can we meet. I think we both have much to

talk about. So much has changed since we last met."
"Yes I agree. Perhaps you should meet Ahmed, you remember him, and a special friend of mine before we see each other" Mohammed suggested in a slightly less than demanding voice.
"Yes of course I remember Ahmed. Ok if you think it's important then I will see your friend. Where and when do you suggest? asked Zadran rapadily wishing to curtail the call.
"Well they are meeting together in the foyer of the Four Seasons Hotel tomorrow at 11 o'clock. Be there and after Ahmed will bring you back to Talaat Harb."

"Very well Mohammed. See you tomorrow" and quickly depressed the close button on the phone.

* * *

The tranquil air of desondency and apathy hanging within the middle-east section of GCHQ was suddenly broken as a beam of esctacy ran across Dean's face the minute he reliased he had picked up the transmission before shouting out at the top of his voice,
"Florence, Florence, oops sorry Miss D'Arcy, I've got him again, I've got Zadran. He is alive and in Cairo!"
Leaping up from her chair Miss D'Arcy ran across to Dean's console to read his handwritten transcript of what he had just overhead.
"First Dean are you sure it was Zadran? How can you be certain?" she asked.
"Well it's obvious. The frequency is 95.62hz but then he even has the stupidity to mention his own name and Mo.." before he could finish,*"Mohammed!! We have him we have the connection with Mr X. we have it!! Fantastic.Well done Dean"* Miss D'Arcy continued,*" Get me a printed copy of the full transcripted echo please Dean asap and I will confirm all this to 'B' (MI6)"* she further requested and

walked back to see Jim Norris who was waiting for her in her office.
"I overheard the good news Florie. This is a brilliant breakthrough" Jim remarked.
"Yes Jim. This time we must get him! and when we do it will satisfy the press and vindicate our tactics and operations over the past few weeks. I will get onto The Home Office straight after I have spoken to Jessica" Florence told Jim with a big grin over her face and breath in her bust.
Following the elated and somewhat lengthy debate to 'B' over the secure line it was agreed in confidence that the follow up to detain Zadran would be a strictly British operation as the premier attack was made on a British aircraft. The Americans would not be invited to participate in the forthcoming Cairo operation, afterall, with the american financial aid still pouring into the Egyptian military machine what could they do anyway. Egypt was far too important a link to the Islamic world for the US to jeopardize, for the sake of taking out one terrorist.

No, The British would go it alone and in a Black Ops covert operation with the MI6 agent Damian Arbuthnot being the key man in Cairo.

Chapter Eight

A Deadly Link Uncovered

It was Jessica Hardman's ('B') authoritative persuasion that convinced the determined Scot, Damian to formulate a rapid plan to either capture or kill the terrorist Abasin Zadran in Cairo but not only that he was to also to establish the identity of the unknown person who would be meeting Ahmed in the Four Seasons Hotel the following day. This character could be very important as it might transpire that another atrocity might be in the planning following the success of the attack at Heathrow.
Damian was given the time and place of the intended meeting with Ahmed with the unknown person and would be left to his own devices to work out a plan. Meanwhile, MI6 with the cooperation of the Ministry of Defence would order a giant RAF C-17 transport aircraft and Chinook helicopter with a full platoon of twenty five SAS paratroopers to standby at the British military base of RAF Akrotiri on the Mediterranean island of Cyprus which is located only around an hour's flying time away from central Egypt for a possible evacuation of Zadran. GCHQ were brought back to full alert status to monitor any further transmissions from Zadran's mobile and to immediately relay their contents directly to Damian ensuring that his intel would be fully current.
With this importance allotted to his sole control Damian began to relish the thought of the possible promotion should he be able to organise a successfull outcome but then with further consideration realised that failure might mean the exact opposite ..he really would have to bring his skills to bear on this assignment.

Being the only agent curently in Cairo, or in Egypt for that matter, his endeavours would need to be thoroughly well planned. Accepting that he had around eighteen and a half hours before the advised meeting at the hotel Damian retired to the comfort of his favourite high back chair to formulate a plan. The mixture of tiredness and a couple of Mackay whiskeys soon relaxed the thirty six year old body into a gentle sleep allowing his thoughts to concentrate.

Out in the world's media several western redtops were calling for blood as retribution for the loss of seven hundred and eighty seven lives whilst the main press of the United States was baiting for an all out war on Syria. Every night on the majority of Europe's TV political shows there was talk of little else than speculation as to who was behind the attack and what would be the best course of retaliatory action. Few were considering talks around a table! All this without knowing who was truely and utterly responsible for the aircraft downing at Heathrow. Neither MI6, GCHQ or The Home Office had thus far released any information regarding the identity of the culprit or the organisation he might have represented.
Denis Morrison and his Cabinet were only too aware as to the damage media speculation might cause with the left papers usually promoting the exact opposite of that of the right. Both Governments were very anxious to be able to proclaim the culprit but not only that but to also to be able to produce him or her in person and with irefutable proof of involvement with the attack so as to riposte any possible compensation for wrongful arrest scenarios by the Human Right's brigade.
When informed of the re-appearance of Zadran The Prime Minister was somewhat relieved that now at last he had a direction in which to concentrate his efforts which could provide an acceptable closure to the Heathrow affair. With

a General Election only fourteen months away Morrison was not wanting to have this unresolved incident hanging over his Government's head ....the ammunition this would provide for the opposition would be too much for him to contemplate.

Following a quiet and relaxed couple of hours light sleep Damian, not fully grasping the reality of the media speculation outside the more pre-occupied internal press of Cairo, was not able to formulate much of a strategy at this stage. All he felt he could do was to observe the meeting at Four Seasons and take a direction from what transpires.
In the meanwhile he would get himself fully prepared for whatever he thought might happen the following day: The two mobile camera phones had to be fully charged, plenty of coinage for possible taxi fares, smart jacket and trousers for the hotel with a spare galabeya (robe) to put over the jacket should he have to follow someone in the street and a gun for protection should trouble come his way.

* * *

At Akrotiri the huge four engined C-17 was rolled out of hanger 6 and stationed on the dispersal pad ready to receive a full load of A-1 fuel, three land Rovers and a Supakat 400 lightly armed all terrain vehicle. The gruesome twin rotor Chinook was already sat there on a rapid dispersment mode, even the two pilots and the load crew were onboard also with a Supakat 400 ready to receive any final orders. Housed in the crew room, fully kitted up studying the terrain maps and possible landing strips in the Sinai Desert should a high-speed operational pick-up of the terrorist Zadran be called for.
The platoon of SAS soldiers led by Lieutenant (Hamish)

McDonald were slowly readying themselves inside the hanger. High Altitude parachutes had been selected by Hamish thinking that an altitude jump from the C-17 might be required for an undetected insertion into Egypt airspace. He also selected the compact MC-51 assault rifle with 7.52 mm rounds for twenty four of his group and himself and two G3SGI's sniper rifles for the last two. With what intel he had received from his Commanding Officer at Hereford McDonald had no real idea of what his mission might involve until communication from the MI6 agent in Cairo had been relayed to him.
As night gently fell on the Mediterranean island the complete task force now sat in limbo awaiting orders with McDonald taking this opportunity to practice a few different moves which could be deemed suitable for a desert scenario with his men.
All was set in Cyprus.

* * *

As usual Damian was again awoken by the gentle **Adhan** call for early morning prayers by the Mu'adhin, echoing melodically around the Egyptian capital. It was just before dawn on the 13th October with the red sun breaking the jagged horizon as Damian pulled back the curtains of his second floor apartment bedroom. His disturbed sleep did nothing to help towards his important day ahead but being the professional that he thought he was, Damian prepared himself as usual by showering and shaving to freshen up. The wall clock read 0855 am as he donned his beige cotton jacket and shemagh before strolling towards the door. It was his deliberate intention to arrive at the Four Seasons very early in plenty of time to see Zadran arrive just in case the he might arrive early and to position himself carefully in the hotel foyer for maximum visual advantage.

The morning air was cool and fresh as the fit and healthy Damian started his walk along Fouad Ln, across Youssef El-Sebaey, down Mohammed Ezz El-Arab, which was congested with several groups of threatening young men obviously planning some form of demonstration and then down Al Bergas to the Nile Corniche where the great river was gently flowing it's course towards the Med. Damian could not help admiring the multitude of white sailed feluccas tacking backwards and forwards attempting to utilise what little wind there was that day.
The main entrance drive into the imposing Four Seasons led from the Nile Corniche, through a security check point and up a gentle slope to the front vestibule doors. Whilst stood outside the main doors Damian took the time to check-in with Mrs Hardman back in London not only to confirm his imminent entry into the hotel but also that MI6 were fully on standby to receive his updates. When completed he then switched off both phones before having a brief look around for any unusual activity or individuals that might require investigating.. nothing.
It was roughly half an hour before Zadran was due to arrive so Damian, carrying an air of subdued authority to blend in with the normal standard of guest expected of a hotel of this calibre, entered the vast foyer to seek out a suitable vantage point from which he could view all the comings and goings. Avoiding eye contact with the three smartly dressed receptionists behind the brown marble counter he headed for one of the sets of high backed chairs grouped around a small marble table on which was placed a folded copy of the "Egyptian Times."
From his seated location the full extent of the foyer and the downstairs bar was visible to the scanning eyes of the MI6 agent who now patiently waited for the various 'guests' to arrive.
The hotel became busy with guests arriving for a business

conference being promoted on the hotel notice board which started to confuse Damian. His watch showed 11am and no obvious suspects drew his attention. Maybe Zadran had changed appearance from the out of focus photograph that Damian had been faxed a few days ago from 'B'. In any event no one coming close to his description seemed to be lurking in the foyer.

Wait, Damian suddenley stiffened up, as in walked a man dressed out of character, wearing a shemagh as well as a pair of dark glasses, with all the other guests and supporting a heavy limp and a crutch under his right arm. His face was tanned and cut in several places and he most definately looked uncomfortable within the surroundings of the salubrious hotel. Instantly Damian knew this to be the terrorist Abasin Zadran and that he was the first westerner to have physically seen him in the flesh!
Without doubt Damian felt a cold aura as Zadran ushered passed him to make his visual sweep of the foyer looking for his old friend Ahmed who at this point was nowhere to be seen. Not wishing to be established as a focal point Zadran casually strolled across to the bar and took up a seat in the corner.
Damian was itching to switch on his mobile and advise London of his sighting but that would only attract attention to himself so resisted and continued to surreptitiously read the 'Times.'
The minutes ticked by... maybe Zadran's contact was not coming or, as is the custom in the middle-east, he would be late. Damian just sat and watched but was nevertheless nervous as he tried to work out a plan should the others not turn up. He decided that he would trail Zadran as he left the hotel and take it from there.

11.19am and with the majority of the delegates now gone to the conference the foyer could almost be called empty.

Zadran looked uncomfortable as he kept on carressing his plastered right leg whilst constantly viewing the entrance doors ...suddenly, with difficulty he stood up and limped towards the reception counter where a middle-aged man dressed in a traditional galabeya accompanied by a smart gentlemen in a suit were standing,

"Salaam Ahmed" he called out.
"Ah! Salaam my friend . How are you?" Ahmed replied whilst gazing at Zadran's crutch *"How did that happen then?"* he inquired.
"Damascus, it's no problem" replied Zadran.
Stepping to one side Ahmed then said,

" I want to introduce you to, Group Captain Richard Barton from Britain. He is here on a clandestine mission with our Brotherhood. Mohammed suggested we all get together as we could all work on our latest and greatest venture."
Barton held out his hand in friendship,
"Good morning Mr Zadran. Mohammed filled me in last night as to your position with Al-Mawla. !" he advised with a certain amount of disgust latently hidden in his voice.
With reticence and concern over being introduced to an English national, especially a militaryman, Zadran grudgingly offered his hand,
"Hello sir."
"Let's go over there and talk" spoke Ahmed pointing to the group of chairs on the far side of the bar.
This would be out of the listening range of Damian's good hearing. All he could do now was to watch and take note of their descriptions and body language.
Ahmed ordered coffee for all three from the barman as they sauntered passed the bar,

"So what is the involvement of this Englishman with your movement Ahmed?" asked Zadran in his Egyptian tongue still not comfortable in the company of his sworn enemy.

Ahmed, who represented the senior level of the Egyptian Brotherhood, was keen to get down to business,Replying in English for Barton to understand,
"Very well Abasin. That I will leave to him to explain but from our point of view we would seek the cooperation of you and Al-Mawla in an important plan that will establish the Brotherhood back in power. Over to you Group Captain."

Clearing his throat the tall, sweet smelling, forty six year old began his explanation,
"Abasin, if I may call you that, you are aware that the Brotherhood were changing the political landscape of Egypt and have just recently been deposed from Government?"
"Yes" replied Zadran.
"Well, I represent a group of disgruntled mercanaries from several European military forces called 'M.A.R.S.' and we have teamed up with Mohammed for an invasion of Israel, we..."

"Israel!!" shouted Zadran.
"Schhhh! Keep your voice down Abasin do you want to world to hear!!"
Damian's acute hearing picked up "Israel". This was valuable intel and wanted to inform 'B' asap but would resist until a safe moment presented itself.
"How the hell do you expect to do that?" asked Zadran with the look of astonishment written across his face. Barton leant forward to within a few inches of Zadran and whispered,
"With a squadron of Tornados and Harriers Abasin!"

Silence, dead silence fell on the trio for what seemed an eternity before Zadran spoke,
"Allah be praised. This get's better and better!!"

Ahmed then took up the conversation,
"Enough in here. The details will be explained to you in full back at HQ now let's just sit back and celebrate Zadran's victorious attack on London the other day with a coffee."
It was with a look of complete shock and awe that the Group Captain took in this revelation,
"So the downing of the two airliners was down to you?" he asked.

"Yes Barton. That was my work. Very good eh!!" Zadran proudly boasted.
"Clever. How on earth did you manage it?" Barton asked.
"Well that was due to my late friend, Asphan Rachid, who sent a cyber virus up the ILS carrier wave to the aircraft." Zadran informed his two colleagues.
Being extremely familiar with aircraft and their electronic approach landing aids Group Captain Barton commented,
"Oh very , very clever Abasin. Well executed."
This information he kept safe in the back of his mind!

On the other side of the foyer Damian Arbuthnot was beginning to feel a little self-conscious having sat there in the same chair for almost an hour reading the same newspaper. He had but little choice than to sit it out and hope that nobody became suspicious. His wait was soon to end as the trio rose from their seats and began walking to the main entrance doors. Damian elected to very carefully follow them.
There were three taxis awaiting pick-ups neatly parked in the hotel's internal rank, the first of which drew up alongside Ahmed and his colleagues as he beckoned the

driver. With it's passengers safely aboard the Mercedes 200SE drove off towards the security check point which was the moment for Damian to jump into the second car and instruct the driver to follow the Mercedes. Is was not far from the hotel to Talaat Harb St with the Mazda 626 driver doing a good job keeping just far enough behind the Mercedes so as not to be noticed ..or so Damian thought! Taking advantage of the solitute in the rear of the Mazda Damian took the opportunity to contact 'B' and quickly convey a progress report with particular mention of Israel.
"Keep with him Damian" 'B' instructed.
Little did Damian notice but the driver was paying particular attention to the conversation as he had been trained in English. All front line Mukhabarat agents (Egyptian secret service), who were scattered throughout the city to surreptitiously listen out for and report back any interesting information they might pick-up, were well versed in several languages. A very high proportion of Cairo taxi drivers were in the employ of the service.
Ahmed's Mercedes drew up outside no. 32 allowing the three passengers to alight onto the pavement and with Zadran limping badly made their way into the building.

Damian did likewise a few seconds later making certain that he knew which floor his suspects were heading for.

Carefully, very carefully he crept up the filthy dirty concrete steps one at a time checking that noboby was observing him as he kept within hearing range to the chatting trio as they approached the second floor. On hearing the slamming shut of a door Damian assumed that they had entered their office so quickened his pace to the assumed door outside of which, leaning at an acute angle on the wall was a nameboard stating ' Embassy of India' which from the state of the door and the surrounding wall, must have been many years ago. Carefully, not wishing to

create a noise by stepping on the rubbish strewn about the floor, Damian laid his left eye to the split in the battered wooden door which gave him a restricted view of the interior of the room. He clearly made out Zadran and the Englishman talking when as to his surprise in walked a man he recognised ..Mohammed (Mr X).
To Damian, he had stumbled upon a hornet's nest of wanted characters all in one place which he figured out to be the headquarters of the now outlawed Egyptian Brotherhood. If only he could call in the SAS now and swoop up the lot he quietly thought to himself.

It was clear from the hand gesticulations of Zadran that not everything was going smoothly which pleased Damian as he felt he might somehow be able to gain an edge from that situation. He heard someone coming up the stairs so quickly and quietly ran up to the next floor and waited, luckily it was yet another visitor for the second floor. The minutes ticked by then, without warning, Damian's mobile rang out it's 'Rule Britania' harmonic. The idiot had forgotton to switch to vibration only after his call to London from the taxi. With the speed and agility of a spingbok gazelle he ran up the next two flights whilst at the same time fumbling in his pocket to retrieve his mobile to switch it off. Fortunately it was not heard in the office above the continual traffic din from the street two floors below entering the open office window.
Further time passed with several raised voices being clearly heard by the patient Mr Arbuthnot, the most predominant of which was that of Mohammed X. Making out the intimate detail of the conversations was a lot more difficult. However several words, such as Tornado, Arish, Bir-Gifgafa, Barton, MARS, Hermes and Israel were clearly transported through the gap in the door and up to Damian now sitting on the cold and filthy step.

Itching to again contact 'B' in London with this knowledge, once more he resisted the temptation to switch on the mobile and to wait for a safer opportunity. The wait would not be long as without warning the office door opened and out walked Zadran with Barton in tow who set off down the stairs into Talaat Harb St. Ensuring the coast was clear Damian himself set off down the stairs in hot pursuit.

It was not until Barton had shut the door of the taxi that Damian noticed a rather shady character, wearing a drab grey coloured Egyptian Galabeya, get into another taxi and pointed toward Barton's car as if to give instructions to his driver to follow in pursuit. Not wishing to loose contact Damian lept into the next Black and White cab that came along. The traffic in the one way street was horrendous which was fortunate as it allowed Damian's driver to keep Barton's taxi in view.
Whilst the taxi was stationary Damian took this opportunity to finally contact 'B' and inform her of the situation,

"Continue observation and report regularly. The SAS are on standby and can be with you in one hour if necessary" Jessica instructed him.

Back in London Jessica had called a meeting in her office with MI5 and Miss. D'Arcy for later that day, so as to be on immediate hand as she suspected something bigger that the incident at Heathrow might well be in the planning. She also thought it prudent to inform the PM as well who insisted on attending the meeting as well.

It was difficult for Damian to understand why Zadran and

Barton drove back to the Four Seasons but they did and entered the hotel together, but they were not alone as the mysterious Egyptian in the galabeya followed close behind. (It turns out that this character was the aptly named Mukhabarat operative, 'Khufu' from Jon Grainge's book "Appointment in Cairo" available on www.blurb.com/user/store/hightrainman)
As Damian cautiously, once again entered the hotel foyer he observed both Zadran and the Group Captain sitting in the same seats as they had previously done earlier that day whilst the agent (Khufu) sat at the bar. Fearing that the situation was now getting somewhat confusing it was to become even more complicated when one of the most beautiful and sexy young ladies he had ever seen walked up to Barton and kissed him full on the lips for all of ten seconds before sitting down to join the duo. Who was this exotic creature sitting there with her dress riding high up her legs? Now Damian was beginning to enjoy this clandestine mission! He knew of no prostitute who would dress like that or kiss like that in Cairo ..she must somehow be involved in whatever mission was going on he thought to himself. Even the Egyptian at the bar must have felt uneasy as he stood up to adjust his robe!

What could be going on?

Chapter Nine

The Final Demise

In his bid to become the world's top terrorist now that Bi-Datan was dead, Abasin Zadran had agreed to collaborate with Mohammed X on his outlandish and crazy plan to invade Israel with the help of M.A.R.S., fronted by Group Captain Dick Barton, and their British fighter jets which were on their way to Egypt as the three of them in the hotel spoke about. In the aftermath of the success of this mission Zadran and his Al-Mawla group of fundamentalists would have a free reign of terror over the remains of the middle-east. The balance of power throughout Europe would change forever ....so thought the madman!
Little did Damian know what a darstardly and far reaching plot he had stumbled upon and no-one to help him save the SAS some one hour's flying time away one the island of Cyprus.
A moment of indecision had crept into Damian's mind .. should he arrange a situation to call in the SAS to deal with Zadran as soon as possible or should he follow up on this newly discovered plot and run the risk of losing him but be on the possible cusp of exposing a bigger plot?. Being the man on the spot, only he could decide. Whilst resting against one the the central marble columns in his bid to remain inconspicuous his mind began to fathom a plan out. He would risk following up on the fermenting plot.

At this point Damian also decided to risk a quick call to 'B' and inform her of his decision so gently slide out of sight around the column and made his call in a gentle voice.

MI6 had little choice than to agree and supporting a sixth sense about the mention of Israel Mrs Hardman suggested to the PM that a full state of military alert, without the knowledge of Egypt, be called at an emergency meeting of NATO. Denis Morrison agreed and further immediately ordered that a further two Squadrons of Typhoon fighter jets and all the C-17's with detachments of paratroopers be sent to Cyprus as a matter of urgency.

The girl stood up and grabbed Barton by the hand beckoning him to follow her. Barton albeit a happily married man with a couple of kids nevertheless took the hint, rose to his feet and bid Zadran farewell agreeing to see him in a couple of days in Sinai. As the couple headed hand in hand towards the elevator, the Egyptian 'Khufu' not wishing to be eyed, turned and buried his head in the bar menu.

Whilst waiting for the elevator to open the girl wrapped her arms around Barton's neck and planted yet another whopper of a kiss upon his lips. It was so obvious to Damian where they were going! so decided to stick with Zadran who had by now also left his seat and was limping his way to the entrance door. Fortunately for Damian the Egyptian decided to take the other elevator to the ninth floor in pursuit of Barton and his escort.

Outside the hotel Zadran hailed another taxi and drove off in his Mazda to the security post for the second time that day. No doubt because the riots in the streets of Cairo had increased during the course of the day the duty guard even searched under Zadran's taxi for bombs as did he when Damian's taxi drew up for inspection a few seconds later.

As the taxi continued in a north-easterly direction in pursuit of Zadran's Mazda Damian recognised

Salah-Salem St and then the airport turn-off as the two cars sped out of Cairo on the Ismailia Road. On and on they drove by-passing the actual town of Ismailia and across the Al-Salam bridge over the Suez Canal into the Sinai Desert on the coastal road heading towards the large Egyptian port of Al-Arish on the Mediterranean coast.

"Sir do you still want me to continue? Your fare is getting very high" the driver asked Damian as he was getting concerned that this might be a hijack.
"No problem. Just keep following that Mazda. Don't worry I have enough money" Damian replied.

One by one the kilometres passed with the sun beginning to fall to the horizon and the desert light darkening to a deep midnight blue.
Soon the silvery sheen of the Mediterranean Sea was visible through the left window with Damian now becoming very concerned as to exactly where they were heading for. Time for another call-in to 'B' with an update, much to the bafflement of the taxi driver whilst praying that the battery would hold out.
On hearing the latest Jessica became concerned to say the least that this new operation might be already underway and had no hesitation in ordering the Chinook with it's complement of SAS troops to immediately get airbourne and fly to the Sinai and await further orders. This she texted to Damian.
Still the Mazda continued along the Al-Kantara Shark highway with nothing but sandunes to the right and water to the left. Eventually the towering cranes of Port Al-Arish came within Damian's eyeline ..now it struck him that the plot he had accidently bumped into was actually in

operation ! He remembered the words he overheard back in No.32, Arish, Israel and Tornado ...then the penny dropped, Tornado!! This was not a wind but a bloody aircraft and of course, the friend of Zadran at the hotel, he looked English with the pale skin and his stature and bearing looked military ..he must be the contact for the aircraft and here he (Damian) was at an Egyptian port near the Israeli border.
"Oh my God!" Damian thought to himself the Tornado fighter plane or planes were coming here to Al-Arish which would explain why Zadran was heading to the waterfront in the port.
Quickly he was onto 'B' again with his revelations.
"No way Damian. You have miscalculated. No way could any Tornado aircraft be on their way to Egypt. There must be another explanation but carry on tailing Zadran. The Chinook will be in your area within minutes" Jessica informed him.
The Mazda, having driven through the town then pulled up on the quayside. Damian instructed his driver to park behind a nearby shed. Having settled the seven hundred and fifty Egyptian pound fare Damian sent his taxi back to Cairo leaving him the freedom to scout around and assess the situation.

* * *

On board the twin engined Chinook helicopter the captain, Flight Lieutenant Dixon, caught a visual on a large container ship flying the Panamanian flag of convenience some one hundred kilometres from the Egyptian coast heading directly for the port at Al-Arish and loaded with at least seventy five huge containers perched on it's decks.. Using his high powered binoculars the co-pilot could just make out the ship's name ...**Hermes**.
Dixon immediately relayed this sighting back to Akrotiri

who then passed it on to MI6 in London. As soon as Jessica ('B') heard of this she immediately sent a 'Flash' message to be relayed to the pilot of the Chinook,

Flash Message to Chinook Pilot

*"On **no** account and I mean **no** account are you to disturb or interfer with the Hermes. You are to remain out of it's visual. Do you understand?"*

signed Director MI6.

Dixon was bewildered as to this instruction but then his was not to reason why but to do and die he muttered and continued on towards Al-Arish reducing his height to three hundred feet above the sea.

* * *

Donning his galabeya to try and blend in should he be spotted Damian removed the fully charged battery from his second mobile phone and inserted into the first so as to portray the same number when he contacted 'B' again, but it was she who rang him just seconds after the battery transfer,

"Damian, listen carefully. The SAS Chinook is only minutes away from you and I want you to arrange to get Zadran away from the main port frontage into a remote location where the SAS can covertly pick him up. Can you do that? I also want you to pick up an enemy rifle or pistol from any conflict and give it to the SAS. Understood!" Jessica commanded.

After a moment's silence Damian responded,

"Ok will do. Advise SAS to pick him up on the road just outside the main port entrance at say" looking at his watch, *"2000hrs. That is just over one hour from now."*

"Very well 2000hrs Damian" 'B' acknowledged.
Now came the difficulty of how to arrange that, Damian thought as he observed Zadran pacing up and down the quayside deep in conversation with a couple of men.

* * *

"*Scrammble, scrammble scrammble"* rang out through the crew room of Al-Mansurah Air Base as the pilots of the QRA (Quick Reaction Alert crew) 7th Fighter Squadron ran to their F-16's to intercept an intruder showing up on the radar as entering Egyptian airspace without authorisation. Within seconds the four single engined F-16's on full afterburners were thundering down 17R before lifting off in a vertical climb to two thousand feet.
A sudden panic broke out in the cockpit of the Chinook as the co-pilot picked up four radar returns heading towards them at high speed.
"Must be Egyptian F-16 interceptors" remarked Dixon *" thought we were low enough to remain undetected! Get onto base and get them removed"* he commanded his co-pilot.Once informed the Akrotiri base commander immediately contacted his opposite number at Al-Mansurah and requested that his fighters break-off in the interests of international cooperation and harmony. It would require an order from central control to concur

advised the Egyptian Commander who immediately made the effort to do so.
Meanwhile the F-16's had located their prey and drew up alongside the Chinnok in a box formation, throttling back to almost idle to stay in formation with the much slower helicopter. The commander switched to international distress frequency,
"Captain of the Chinook. This is Commander Burak of the Egyptian Air Force. I advise you to alter course to 000 degrees and head out of Egyptian airspace or I will have too shoot you down."
Seconds passed before Dixon replied,
"Commander, this is the captain of the Chinook. You will shortly be receiving orders to break off as our mission is on a humanitarian basis so please depart in peace."
"Chinook captain you will fly a circular holding pattern until that order comes through please Sir" the lead F-16 pilot ordered. For three and a half minutes the five aircraft flew a three kilometre circle until the silence in the F-16 cockpit was broken with the order from his base,
"Break off and return to base F-16 Commander" and with that the four fighter jets broke formation, engaged their afterburners and left the Chinook in a thunderous roar of black smoke.
"That was close Sir" spoke Dixon's co-pilot.

Whilst the Flight Lieutenant agreed he confidently knew the fighters would not endanger the overall mission and resumed his heading towards Al-Arish whilst further reducing height down to two hundred feet above the calm dark water.

The remaining distance to a safe landing site which Dixon established to be around a kilometre from the port entrance did not take long to travel before the Lycoming engines set the mighty Chinook down in an enormous cloud of dust and sand behind a row of neatly planted palm trees on the eastern edge of the town. No sooner than the weight of the helicopter was taken up by it's hydraulic undercarriage than the rear doors opened allowing the SAS to drive the Supakat 400 all terrain vehicle out and ready it for the drive to the port. All guns were cocked and the 400 machine gun installed and loaded. All was set for the dash to pick up Zadran at 2000hrs ..some twenty minutes time.

In his impatience waiting for the MV Hermes with it's cargo to arrive Zadran lit up a cigarette giving away his exact location to Damian in the falling darkness. This gave Damian his idea: Taking the Sig Sauer P230 pistol from his pocket and remaining hidden, he aimed at the sky and fired one shot skyward. This immediately caught the attention of Zadran and his two cohorts. Zadran stamped out his cigarette before all three sought cover in the nearby shed.
In line with Damian's guess Zadran ordered his two colleagues to go and investigate the area from where the shot was heard. Anticipating their arrival Damian had taken cover behind a convenient stock of forty five gallon oil drums. It was difficult for him to hear the two men coming in their soft sandals but their sillouettes showed against the moonlight sky allowing Damian to judge when they were approaching the drums. As, together the two suspects passed, Damian jumped out behind them striking the first hard on the back of his head with the butt of the Sauer sending him to the ground and as the other turned round then brought his gunhand rapidly upwards catching the suspect clean on the lower jaw with the pistol barrel. Both suspects were out cold on the floor. Another hard blow to each of their heads with the butt of the Sauer made certain they would not be troubling Damian again! and now for Zadran.
Damian waited, hidden in the dark and waited and waited

knowing that Zadran's curiosity would get the better of him and would come to investigate what happened to his friends. The nervous wait continued with Damian's watch now showing 1942hrs.

The SAS commander realising the time ordered his six men aboard the Supakat and off they sped across the compacted desert terrain towards the port entrance at full throttle trailing a cloud of dust.

Zadran could wait no longer. With the imminent arrival of the ship he broke cover to investigate the silence by the shed where his friends seemed to have disappeared. The limping sillouette was easy for Damian to spot ..the bait had been taken.

The sight of the two dimly lit bodies lying prostrate on the ground immediately raised Zadran's adrenalin rate and alertness as Damian arose from the shadows of the drums and shouted,

"Put up your hands Zadran or I will kill you!!!"

With the reaction of a trapped wild animal Zadran turned around bringing his crutch upwards at an alarming rate taking Damian completely by surprise as it hit his gun arm throwing the Sig Sauer pistol to the ground. Zadran's instinctive action threw him temporary off balance which gave Damian the chance to land a sharp left jab to his lower jaw sending Zadran to the ground in a spray of dust. Quickly bending down and grabbing the gun Damian attempted to take the upper hand but suddenly his legs were taken from under him by Zadran's feet. Both men were now on the ground however Damian proved to be the fitter and quicker of the two as he was the first to his feet and able to give Zadran a really swift and extremely hard kick in the stomach winding Zadran before he could rise. Followed by another kick, this time to the groin, Zadran was out cold with agony. Damian had him at his mercy but

Supakat 400 all terrain vehicle

had only a few minutes left to get him to the entrance gate so with an inordinate amount of difficulty he slung the limp, but semi-conscious, Egyptian body over his muscular Scottish shoulder and started walking with difficulty towards the port gates.

The SAS team now entered the outer area of the town but with the riots in Cairo having been televised across Egypt the local people of Al-Arish seemed not to be aroused by the sight of an armed military vehicle speeding through their streets.
As Damian, now severly weakened having carried the dead weight on his shoulder for around four hundred metres across barren ground to avoid being seen, was grateful of the sight of the entrance gates before him. Passing through them to the other side of the road Damian prepared to

dump the body on the verge which unfortunately for him gave Zadran the chance to overpower Damian and punch him hard in the face drawing blood in the process. Not satisfied with just one punch and wanting to get back to receive the ship (Hermes), now due to arrive, Zadran embarked on a series of further punches to Damian's face and body. One punch after another causing much bloody damage to the once good looking Damian Arbuthnot who now fell to the ground. The angry Zadran who had had his dignity as the leader of Al-Mawla insulted just kept on kicking the MI6 agent in the stomach with his good leg.

Caught in the headlights on the oncoming Supakat 400 the driver and several of the soldiers aboard saw the beating in the road and realising that it had to be Zadran, prepared to jump from the vehicle to arrest the assailant. One after another the five soldiers, along with Colonel Anderson, jumped to the road from the moving vehicle and ran towards Zadran, who being taken completely by surprise, had no choice than to surrender with his hands held high in the air.

As rehearsed through their rigorous training the soldiers rapidly and roughly pinned Zadran to the ground, spread his legs and searched him for weapons then held him at gunpoint whilst the medically trained Sergeant attended to the severely wounded Damian agonising in acute pain on the verge.
Diagnosing that Damian had three broken ribs, a broken nose and a damaged spleen all of which required attention in a hospital at the earliest opportunity Anderson decided to take Damian back to Cyprus along with Zadran.
Ordering everyone back aboard the Supakat Colonel Anderson himself jumped into the front seat and commanded the driver to about turn and return to the Chinook with all haste.

It was just as the Supakat was half-way through it's turn that a blast and the consequent fragmentation from an RPG (Rocket Propelled Grenade) caught Anderson full in the face ripping the head from the body in an instant!
"Fucking arseholes! What the hell was that ?" shouted one of the soldiers.
"We are under attack from that jeep over there" cried out one of the other soldiers pointing further up the road.
"Let's make a run for it !" shouted the medic.*"No stand and fight!"* cried the soldier as he opened up the roof mounted machine gun sending five hundred bullets at the hostile jeep few of which hit the vehicle in the dark.
Then a second explosion landed just behind the back wheels blowing the Supakat onto it's side spewing it's passengers over the road.
"Get behind the car for cover!" ordered a soldier which instinctively they all did dragging Damian and Zadran with

Chinook HC3 helicopter

them. With the Supakat on it's side the machine gun was useless aside from the fact that it had been bent in the blast.
Another blast landed to their rear, fortunately causing no casualties.
"Who the hell are these bastards?" asked a soldier.
"They are my brothers. I cannot be allowed to be captured alive. Allah will protect me" spoke Zadran.

Soon another rebel jeep joined the first and launched a third grenade, which further damaged the Supakat.
"What do we do now?" asked a soldier.
"Quick, grab the Colonel's radio headset from the head over there on the road and call in the Chinook" replied another soldier.
"Great Fred go and get it then as it was your idea" suggested Private Riley.
"Chinook captain come in, come in" spoke Fred.
"Chinook here. Go ahead"
"We are incapacitated, Colonel Anderson is dead and we are taking enemy fire. Come and rescue!" requested Fred.
"Hang on we are on our way. Be there in five" advised Dixon as he ignited the Lycoming T55 burners. The engines burst into life with the rotors gradually beginning to rotate. Within a few seconds the aircraft was lifting from the ground with it's usual thracking noise pervading the area.

"Booom!! as yet another shell exploded close to the overturned Supakat followed by rapid machine gun fire from at least ten hand held machine guns. The rebels were making an advance upon the British soldiers.

From the cockpit Flight Lieutenant Dixon and his co-pilot could clearly see the gunflashes in the dark distance providing a landmark to head for.

Exchanging fire the rebel Brotherhood made ground on the British SAS group coming within a few metres of their stronghold behind the vehicle. Taking many casualties was acceptable for either the recovery or extinction of the Al-Mawla leader so continued to push forward.
Thud! as an SAS soldier gets hit in the right arm and keels over in agony. Thud! as another takes a bullet in the head. He's gone.

It was looking like the end was close for the brave Brits but then the welcome sound of the oncoming twin rotors thracking in the air became louder and louder as the huge helicopter came into view at virtually ground level.
On seeing this monster rapidly approaching the rebels directed all their available fire at it in fear! Fortunately for the two pilots the armourplated windscreen held as several bullets struck but failed to break through.
This gave the remaining SAS soldiers the chance to break cover and let loose with their machine guns taking out several rebels but it was the two M134 7.62mm miniguns aboard the Chinook that opened up at two thousand five rounds per minute that obliterated the rebel attack. Strafing the ground with these gatling guns torn the road to pieces including the rebels and their two jeeps. Following a ten second burst nothing, absolutely nothing was left! The fight was over.
Dixon brought the helicopter to the ground whilst opening the rear doors giving entry to the SAS, their wounded and dead plus Zadran and Damian. Colonel Anderson's head was quickly scooped up and bundled into a sack for a later burial with the remains of his body.
"What about the wounded rebels?" asked the co-pilot.
"Leave the buggers to rot "replied Dixon.
Once the SAS group were safely aboard, the Chinook rose to the air in an almighty cloud of dust and debris before

heading back out to sea out of Egyptian airspace.
The world's most wanted terrorist was now safely in the custody of British hands. Once 'B' was informed in London a sense of relief hung over the department .... now the PM could announce a closing to the Heathrow incident.

But what was to become of Zadran??

Concentrating on holding a steady five hundred feet and one hundred and thirty kts over the sea on a heading of zero one zero degrees some fifty or so kilometers from the coast, plus recovering from the stress of the engagement both Flight Lieutenant Dixon and his co-pilot failed to observe the rapidly depleting fuel level in the rear tank. It did however come to their notice when the red low fuel warning red began to flash.
"Sir we have a low fuel warning" remarked the co-pilot.
"Impossible we were full when we left base" Dixon advised.
"We must have taken a hit !" remarked the co-pilot.
"Do we have enough in the forward tank to get us to Cyprus?" Dixon asked.
Following a quick bit of mental arithmetic using the fuel consumption tables for the Lycoming T55 engine and reading the DME (Distance Measuring Equipment) the co-pilot advised ... *"No!"*
"Ok so what are our options?" asked Dixon as a slight trembling began in his hands.
"Well sir. We could divert to Israeli territory or we could hunt for an aircraft carrier cruising in these waters or we can ditch" continued the co-pilot.*"Israel is off limits, orders from above. This baby floats but not for long. Give a broadcast for any shipping then."*

The broadcast and communication with Akrotiri base brought no results for any shipping within range which left Flight Lieutenant with only one option,

"Gentlemen we are left with no other choice than to head back to Egypt and call for a pick-up, so that's what we do" stated Dixon as he altered the Chinook's heading to one nine zero degrees and called up Akrotiri,
"Akrotiri Command this is Chinook Alpha one. We are heading back to Sinai request pick-up, will activate homer."
"Alpha one. It will be arranged . Make it a desolate spot if possible sir."

With haste the base commander called a scrammble for two Chinook's with a complement of twenty commandoes in each to head due south to Sinai. He further ordered three Typhoon fighter jets to take to the sky in an hour's time to fly south and give a patrolling cover to the pick-up. Within ten minutes both the mighty Chinooks were airbourne and speeding south on full power anxious to rescue their colleagues stranded in the Sinai Desert.
"I suggest we make for the north-eastern strip of Lake Bardawil, sir. Looks a deserted area and we can comfortably make it" the co-pilot suggested as he folded his map of Egypt into a more manageable size.
"Very well prepare the boys down the back " ordered Dixon *"and handcuff Zadran, both arms and legs. We don't want any trouble from him when we are on the ground."*
Fully realising the situation Zadran then intervened,
"Allah be praised. So we are going back then. My men we cut you into little pieces and feed you to the dogs for treating me like this" he shouted at the top of his voice and spat a huge blob of sputum into the soldiers face as he closed the handcuff tight around Zadran's hands.
"Gag him as well Goeff. Keep the bastard quiet."
"How is the MI6 boy?" asked Flight Lieutenant Dixon.
The medic came up to the flight deck with his report,

"Sir , the English guy needs treatment. He has been badly beaten and may not pull through. I do not have the skills to do any more for him."
"Ok do your best to keep him comfortable, could get a bit rough shortly" advised Dixon and now fully aware of his situation concentrated on locating the lake and picking out a suitable landing spot.
The unwelcome sight of the dark Egyptian coastline came into the pilot's view fairly quickly so Dixon ordered all lights out so as not to be spotted from the ground and there shimmering in the moonlight was the enormous seventy kilometre long lake.
Once again the thracking rotor blades powered by the Lycoming engines could be heard through the silent night air of the Sinai Desert so Dixon was very keen to set the machine down with the greatest haste and shut down the engines.
"How's the fuel?" Dixon asked.
"Just enough left sir. We should be good. How about that sandbar over there" the co-pilot pointed out.
"You mean that narrow one right on the coastline."
"Yes sir."
"Yeah that looks good. Plenty of open space to see anyone coming and easy for the rescue aircraft to get in and out quickly. We'll go for it" ordered Dixon so lowered the undercarriage in preparation for the landing on the barrier.
The still windless evening air allowed Dixon to put the Chinook's nose toward the sea with the fusealge across the sandbar thus offering maximum protection for the crew and SAS soldiers in the unfortunate event of an assault by ground troops.
The wheels sat deep and snug in the soft, marshy sand as the Lycoming engines spooled down for the last time then Dixon, now being the senior officer, jumped from his seat

issuing orders for the all able bodied men to get armed and set up a defence shield around the helicopter to await the arrival of the rescue aircraft.
With the defence arrangements fully in place and the two M134's strategically located at either end of the aircraft Flight Lieutenant Dixon activated the long-range homing device and readied the Chinook's self-destruct, the timer of which would be activated the moment the rescue force arrived. There could be no chance of the Chinook or any of it's sensitive equipment onboard being allowed to fall into the hands of the Brotherhood or any other terroristic organisation so it would have to be completely and utterly destroyed.
They were down safely and ready for action should it come.All was ready for the rescue so there was nothing more to do than to be patient and wait.

* * *

"I have it sir, I have the homing signal of Alpha one. Alter heading to one nine five degrees" advised Flying Officer Bentham who was the co-pilot of the lead rescue Chinook. The two ship formation presently around forty minutes flying time from the Sinai altered course whilst reducing altitude to a low two hundred feet above the shimmering sea.
The lead ship commander, Flight Lieutenant "Ace" Wright, an experienced Chinook aerobatic demo pilot, who was looking forward to the possibility of some action as he was suffering from withdrawal symptoms since the completion of his wild two year tour in Afghanistan, called for the manning of the two M134's and each to be fitted with the maximum five thousand round belts. That would give a minutes continuous fire ensuring total annihilation of anything unfortunate enough to be in it's path.

"Everything ready sir" reported Bentham.

"Fine. Let's go get our boy's back" uttered Wright.

* * *

The still evening desert air began to chill the crew as the temperature dropped to not far above zero requiring those outside to seek their combat jackets stowed in the aircraft. Not a sound could be heard from the entrenched crew, the odd flamingo squall and rippling of the sea was all that broke the night silence.
"Any sign of activity on the scope?" Dixon called to his co-pilot as he was busy ensuring all the gear was packed and ready to be transported to the incoming aircaft.
"No sir, nothing yet" advised the Flying Officer.
Having completed the packing, Dixon thought to take advantage of the quiet spell and have a chat with Zadran whose hands were gradually going knumb with the tightness of the handcuffs. After carefully removing the gag Dixon sat beside Zadran and began talking,
"So why did you do it?" he asked.
This being, apart from Barton, his first encounter with his adversary from the west Zadran replied with venom and hate in his broken English speech,
"Why you enter Iraq and Afghanistan then want bomb Syria? You invaders. You enemy to Islam and good name of Allah! You ..."
"Bullshit, utter bullshit man. Were you involved with the bombing of the New York towers?" Dixon angrily interrupted.
"You never know!" replied Zadran as his spat into Dixon's face.

Wiping the dripping sputum from his face with his handkerchief Dixon continued,
"So you were responsible for the Heathrow job then?"
Zadran sat silent.
Dixon again spoke,
"Your silence tells me everything arsehole" then pressing his hand hard onto Zadran's right (broken) leg causing Zadran extreme pain Dixon asked again. Zadran's response was predictable as he rapidly regurgitated a huge amount of sputum and plastered it clean into Dixon's face which angered him to the point of him landing a 'cool' right-hander to Zadran's jaw.
Reeling back with the pain in his right knuckle Dixon saw Zadran slump forward , out cold!
Again silence reined over the stranded group for a short while until the crack of a rifle shot rang out hitting one of the soldiers in the head who fell to the ground ..dead.
"Everybody down we are under attack!" shouted one of the few remaining soldiers as several more shots rang out, several of which hit the airframe.

Appearing out of the darkness the outermost SAS soldier saw several shapes running towards him so unleased a few rounds from his Accuracy AW50 sniper rifle taking out three of the assailants who fell to the ground. The remaining two managed to get to the soldier without being shot and entered into a hand to hand combat with him. In anticipation of this the soldier had withdrawn his 6" shoulder holster knife and embedded it into one of the assailant's belly before receiving a rifle butt in his own face. Just as the final assailant was about to shoot the wounded SAS soldier as he lay bleeding profusely on the ground, one of his colleagues saw the incident and shot the assailant clean between the eyes with his Sig Sauer pistol. The attack was over for the moment.

* * *

"Akrotiri tower to Typhoon Bravo Squadron. You are cleared to take-off. Wind zero one zero at five kts."
"Bravo, take-off 010" repeated Wing Commander Grainge as he thrust his throttle levers fully forward and engaged afterburners. The silent Cypriat night suddenly was awakened with the thunderous roar of two Eurojet EJ200's pumping out forty thousand pounds of thrust, lifting the Typhoon FGR4 vertically into the air to level out at five thousand feet. The other three followed behind in close formation.
Flying time to Egypt would be no more than twenty five minutes.
"Typhoon Bravo to Rescue one over" called Grainge.
"*Rescue one here. Go ahead"* replied Wright.
"Typhoon Bravo is airbourne. ETA your zone twenty two minutes" the Typhoon commander stated.
"Rescue one. We have just made visual on Alpha one (Dixon) who is in engagement under fire. Going in now" advised Wright.
"Call for ordnance if you deem necessary as that can be with you in seconds" confirmed Grainge.
"Will do. Rescue one out."
"We are now entering Egyptian airspace, crew" advised 'Ace' Wright, *"So be on the ball Gentlemen."*
With the beady eyes of F/O Bentham having just caught view of several bright but small flashes dead ahead and then a much larger one,
"Must be them sir. Look's like they are still under attack."
"Righty ho in we go then" rallied Wright itching to get involved as he opened the rear doors in anticipation of a rapid in/out.

The familiar and most welcomed thracking of two rotor blades grew in intensity as the Chinook approached into the frey whilst the other Chinook stood off ready to strike if 'Ace' could not handle the situation.

The small advancing group of Brotherhood rebels were also aware of an incoming aircraft so pressed ahead with their advance having used their intelligence to have worked out that their partner in crime could be on board the stranded helicopter, either dead, wounded or alive and they wanted him back.

An RPG landed to the rear of the stranded Chinook kicking up an enormous spray of mushy sand covering the bottom door in six inches of sand. On the good side ..no one got hurt. Then another hit the forward rotor throwing one of the huge blades into the air which landed vertically in the waters shallow edge. There it majestically stood, upright like a monument of remembrance in the Sinai Desert.
Several bullets hit the incoming Chinook's bullet proof windscreen which put 'Ace' Wright in the mood for a high incidence landing but not before he had unleashed both belts of his M134's into the darkness below. The devastation to the landscape was difficult to describe: palm trees cut in half and craters carved in the sand but more depressingly, bits and pieces of several Egyptian bodies left strew over the sandbar with the near lake turned red with a deluge of Egyptian blood.
Coming in at eighty kts over the sea Wright brought the nose of the Chinook to a near vertical stop before levelling out as he attempted a high speed tactical landing bringing the aircraft down to a hover at one foot above the ground thus avoiding sinking into the sand. No orders were necessary for all the soldiers to gather up their belongings, pick up the casualties, including Damian Arbuthnot and

scrammble as fast as they could into the hovering Chinook. Meanwhile Dixon activated the self destruct timer located in the flight deck, slung the limp body of Zadran over his shoulder and ran through the open rear doors of his Chinook and into those of 'Ace's'.
Slinging Zadran down as if a sack of potatoes on the aluminum floor he then ran to the flight deck to advise the captain that everyone to be accounted was for onboard. That was enough for Flight Lieutenant Wright to wind open the Lycoming throttles , raise the tail to a sixty degree angle and push the aircraftt forward gattering enough forward speed to then raise the nose and climb out in a near vertical climb to relative safety at one thousand feet. Back on the sandbar the remaining rebels, having emptied their magazines at the departing helicopter, took the opportunity to enter the sad and lonely but stranded Alpha one Chinook in the hope of some possible gain from any forgotton intelligence or personal momentoes. As the destruct timer hit zero an almighty ball of flame travelled the entire length within the aircraft engulfing the Egyptian rebels in a living hell before the H.E. explosion finally blew the Chinook HC3 into a million pieces.
"Fucking hell! that was close" cried out Bentham as 'Ace' Wright and all those on board his Chinook felt the blast wave whilst in the climbout to team up with the second Chinook.

The ball of flame rising high into the night sky was easily visible to Wing Commander Grainge in the lead Typhoon now just a few kilometers from the Egyptian coast,
"Typhoon Bravo to Rescue one. Saw the blast. What's the score?" requested Grainge.
"Rescue one. We are ok and back at height heading home" replied Wright.

"Sir, sir we have four high speed bogies at two o'clock!"

rang out the pilot of the second Typhoon.
"Shit must be the bloody yipo F-16's out of Al-Mansurah!" shouted Grainge, *"Better contact them to save an incident"* he advised his second pilot.
"Commander of F-16 interception group this is Commander Grainge of RAF Typhoon group. Sorry to have entered your airspace. Our mission is complete and returning home. Appreciate your cooperation. Good night sir" and prompty turned his Typhoon Squadron through one hundred and eighty degrees and headed back to Cyprus, somewhat disappointed in not having the chance of an engagement.

Receiving the message, Commander Burak in his F-16 felt uneasy at the thought of tangling with four vastly superior Typhoons which would inevitably result in certain death for him and his colleagues let alone lead to an international incident for Egypt,
"Typhoon commander. This is Egyptian F-16 commander, no harm done. Have a good trip home sir" Burak spoke before turning about to return to Al-Mansurah.

Immediately Chinook Rescue one landed at Akrotiri and followed the instructions from the tower to continue the short taxy to the dispersal pad where a reception committee comprising of twenty five fully armed RAF Regiment soldiers and their commanding officer had been ordered to meet it. Sensing there could be a little trouble ahead Wright shut down both engines and opened the rear doors. The Regiment team surrounded the helicopter allowing none of it's occupants to vacate the aircraft.
A military ambulance closely pursued by a jeep, with a canvas rear canopy , drew up alongside the Regiment officer and awaited instructions.

'Ace' Wright was the first to appear at the rear entrance of

Rescue one,
"Please stay aboard sir for the time being. We will be needing to take your 'special' passenger off first if you will bring him here please" ordered the officer.
"This is ridiculous sir !" spoke Wright and stepped off the ramp onto the concrete. Instantly all twenty five soldiers raised their rifles to the hip! which brought Wright to an immediate halt with his hands held high above his head,
"Ok , ok!" and begrudgingly stepped back onto the ramp to arrange for Zadran to be brought out.
As Zadran limped onto the concrete two of the soldiers grapped his arms and led him to the rear of the jeep which promptly sped off with Zadran and the two soldiers sitting in the back out of sight.
"Ok Flight Lieutenant you can all come out now and stand here please" ordered the officer who incidently was of a senior rank than 'Ace'.
"I have several injured and a couple of dead bodies aboard" Wright informed the officer.
"Very well please take them to the ambulance and we will take very good care of them" the officer commanded.
The injured Damian was the first into the ambulance followed by the walking wounded SAS boys followed by the bodies.
"The rest of you will come with us please" ordered the officer as his Regiment gathered around the twenty five or so remaining crew and soldiers and escorted them to the nearby hanger. Once inside the group were shown to a comfortable holding area normally reserved for visiting aircrew of VIP flights.
"You will all remain in here in a form of quarantine Flight Lieutenant until the future of your fugitive has been decided. London is anxious not to let the world and especially the media, know of his capture. Do you understand sir?"
With no choice at hand Wright answered,

"Of course."
Damian was feeling much more comfortable having now having had professional attention to his damaged ribs and spleen in the base hospital but was a bit concerned as to why two armed guards were permanently placed at his bedside. Having made an inquiry from the doctor he was informed that it was in protection of him openly talking about the terrorist that he was instrumental in bringing back to Cyprus. Damian understood the delicacy of the situation and relaxed into a slumber.
Having been incarcerated in the darkened room within the main holding area of Akrotiri Air Base, Zadran lay stricken on the concrete floor, devoid of water and food awaiting his fate, still in handcuffs.

* * *

Back in the early morning London sunshine the PM, now more relaxed in the knowledge of the capture and consequent holding of the Egyptian terrorist who, having had considerations with the Cabinet in Downing Street, instructed The Home Secretary to contact MI6 ('B') and order her to Cyprus with immediate haste.Once settled back in her Whitehall Office Fiona Campbell closed the office door and called Jessica Billgate-Hardman on the scrammbled line.
"Good Morning Hardman here."
"Good morning Jessica, Fiona. I have just returned from a Cabinet meeting and the PM wants you and your interrogation team to fly immediately to Cyprus. There is an RAF BA146 standing by at RAF Northholt for imminent departure so get your team downthere within the hour please. You will be handed your directive when

onboard. Are you clear Jessica?" instructed The Home Secretary.
"Yes I understand Ma'am" and before she could replace the receiver billowed out for Lt. Col. Hayward.
The journey to Northolt, located only six miles east of Heathrow on the A40 Western Avenue, in the official Jaguar XJ with her hastily gathered team of Lt. Col. Hayward and his two professional, what could only be considered as thugs, had soon passed as they reported in at the main gate.
With a brief review of their papers complete the car was directed to the holding pad where the four engined executive jet painted in dull Air Force grey stood waiting with all engines running. Once the small team was safely aboard, strapped in their leather seats and the door closed the pilot commenced his taxiing for an immediate easterly departure for Cyprus. The outward departure took the aircraft directly over London before altering course to zero four five to overfly Paris and onward to Akrotiri.
Having trimmed out at flight level 30 and handed control of over to his co-pilot, the 146 captain walked back to the cabin to seek out Mrs Jessica Hardman. Having established her identity he handed her a brown A4 envelope with

"TOP SECRET" written across it and underneath

"For Your Eyes Only" **Mrs J.Billgate-Hardman**

"Good morning Ma'am. I have been asked to personally give this to you."
"Ah yes, thankyou I have been told to expect this. Incidently what is our anticipated flight time to Cyprus captain?"
"Approximately four hours and twenty minutes Ma'am depending on wind" the pilot replied.

Carefully Jessica opened the officially sealed envelope and removed the single sheet of quality A4 paper. It read:

TOP SECRET

From: Prime Minister UK

To: Mrs J. Billgate-Hardman MI6

Contents---Orders

"For Your Eyes Only"

On no account to be shown to anyone else

Subject: ***Abasin Zadran***

Mrs Billgate-Hardman

You and your team have been sent to interrogate Abasin Zadran. On no account are you to be persuaded by the American Services for this prisoner to be transported to Guantanamo Bay. He is to be questioned, by you, at Akrotiri to obtain information about his Al-Mawla organisation, his connection with the Twin Towers and Heathrow incident and contacts in the United Kingdom.
You will have 24 hours from when you arrive in Cyprus in which to do this.

After this time the prisoner whether he released information or not is to be disposed of and **never** to be found.
On ***no account*** is anyone outside your team to ever know about the contents of this letter or be made aware of the interrogation or demise of the prisoner.

You will shread the letter upon being read.

The order was signed personally by the Prime Minister.

'B' read the order several times to ensure she fully understood it's contents. In all her years with the Service she had never received an order like this before and wanted to be certain as to it's magnitude.
Calling for one of the stewards she requested the wherabouts of the shreader,
"It's down at the rear ma'am. Pulls out of the bottom drawer" he replied. With that job done she returned to her seat for a quiet sleep.
The flight passed without incident and before the team knew it they were on the final approach into Akrotiri Air Base, then with a small bump the 146 touched down on 10R and engaged reverse thrust. As the engines wound down and the door opened at dispersal one of the base's jeeps drew up to collect it's passengers and immediately transport them to the holding cells.

The base commander was at the main holding entrance to greet Mrs Hardman and her specialist group ,
"Welcome but on this occasion we will do without the preliminaries. Do you want to see the prisoner now?" he asked.

"Could do with a wash up first though" she replied, *"then we will get to our business. I want you to be certain that we are not going to be disturbed once we start our interview. Do you fully understand?"* Mrs Hardman told the Group Captain.
"Yes of course. I will place a heavy guard on this door just to make sure."
"Good. I will also need a forty five gallon drum full of water and the use of the plane and crew that brought Zadran back from Egypt to be at my disposal in 24hrs for an hour or so" she further informed the base commander.
"Are you going to do what I think you are?" the Group Captain asked with concern.
"That is none of your business Group Captain! Now please show me to a washroom! then can you take me to see Damian Arbuthnot."
The sight of one of her entrusted agents lying in a hospital bed with a heavily bruised face and strapping around his waist did not best please her and would help in her quest to obtain information from the man responsible for these injuries. With the short private conversation complete and in possession of the details of the what finally happened at Al-Arish, Jessica Hardman made her way back to the holding centre to embark her team on the ugly task of interrogating the world's most wanted jihadist.

Hayward had already prepared the room in which the large drum, full to the brim with clean and very cold water, stood in the middle. Devoid of any other furniture except for a carver chair the empty, windowless room whose ambient temperature was deliberately contained at near zero degrees, awaited it's special guest.
With one of the 'thugs' holding each of Zadran's arms he was dragged from his holding cell into the room and forcibly sat in the chair. For the next five minutes not a

word was spoken. With the room's door closed silence reined. This was standard MI6 interviewing policy to give the prisoner plenty of opportunity to talk without any coercion being applied. Most interviewees crack at this stage ..but not the hardened Zadran.

Lt. Col. Hayward having paced up and down the room for the entire period of silence then broke into his broken attempt at Egyptian ,

"Mr Zadran, you have admirably demonstrated your resilience which is to be respected, however, none of us will be leaving this room until I have the answers to a few very simple questions the first of which is were you involved in the destruction of the twin towers in New York?"

Silence

"I ask once more. Were you involved in the twin towers destruction?" spoke Hayward.

Again silence for ten seconds before Zadran felt the first of the three punches to his jaw from one of the thugs. With blood trickling from his mouth Zadran still remained silent. Three move punches were impacted. Still silence from Zadran.

Hayward then changed his question,

"Ok let's try another question. Were you behind the atrocity at Heathrow Airport ?"

Again silence.

"Very well have it your way!" confirmed the angry Hayward returning to his natural English and clicking his fingers at the two thugs who understood it's meaning and immediately plunged Zadran's head into the water, holding it there for forty seconds as by Hayward's watch.

Gasping for breath with water dripping heavily from his face Zadran began to utter a few words in Egyptian,

"Do what you like. I will go to heaven covered in glory!"

"So you were behind Heathrow! thankyou."

All this procedure was being videoed by the second thug in the hope that it would record positive confidential evidence of Zadran's involvement in terroristic activites, should it be required in the future.
"I did not say that!" interrupted Zadran.
"Then say it now !!" shouted Hayward in his voluminous voice.
"Do as you will. I shall be welcomed in Heaven for my deeds. Allah be praised" uttered Zadran.
The black hood was forcibly placed over Zadran's head by the first thug before smashing him twice more in the face with an old fashioned knuckle duster.
A profuse amount of blood began ouzing from under the hood.
"How did you carry out the Heathrow incident? Who were your accomplices?" continued Hayward.
"Go to hell !" responded Zadran before his head was again pushed into the drum of water ..this time for seventy five seconds.
Struggling for air inside the soaking hood Zadran fell back into the chair in a semi-unconscious state. Without allowing for any recovery time Hayward persisted in asking his questions. Time and again the performance was repeated but to no avail.
Finally running out of patience Hayward called for Zadran to be cuffed to the arms of the chair, the hood to be removed, the chair to be tipped backwards almost to the horizontal and a towel to be placed fully over Zadran's face.
"One more time, who are your colleagues and where are they?" Hayward demanded.
Silence.
Obeying the signal from Hayward the second thug collected the metal jug and filled it with water from the drum. The first thug knew what was about to happen,

"Sir you cannot do this. It's out of the Geneva Convention an......" but before he could finish Mrs Hardman hastily intervened,
"I will take full responsibility. This is my decision, continue Lt. Col. I want answers. We have only a few hours left" she demanded.
"No ma'am I cannot be a party to this" the thug informed the room and walked out into the fresh Cypriat air.
"Continue Hayward" ordered Jessica.
The remaining thug then started slowly pouring the water onto the towel which became soaked, very soaked. Within seconds Zadran's body began to wriggle and twitch as he gasped for non-existent air beneath the wet towel. The towel remained over his face for one and a half minutes with the wriggling growing in intensity.
"Take it off" ordered Hayward.
Taking in huge gulps of air Zadran gradually recovered.
"Once again, who are your colleagues?" demanded Hayward in his elevated voice, who then received the customary blob of Egyptian sputum in the face from Zadran.
"Again!!" commanded the Col.
"Sir are you sure?" asked the thug appealing to the better nature of his boss as he too was becoming concerned of this waterboarding treatment.
Once again Hrs Hardman stepped in with complete authority,
"Carry on soldier. That is an order from the highest level. Do you understand me?"
Afeared of the consequence of disobeying orders, especially from such a high level officer as 'B', he reluctantly continued to pour more water onto the towel.

Again the body wriggled and wriggled and wriggled, *"Allah be praised"* came from underneath the towel. The wriggling intensified to a dramatic level then ..... the body suddenly slumped. The aspiration of Vomitus into Zadran's lungs finally drowned him..... Abasin Zadran was **dead.**!
"Shit, shit Colonel you have gone too far " yelled
Mrs Hardman *"What the fuck I am going to tell the PM!!"*

Taking what little remained of the day to consult with Damian and to think things through in the warm Cypriat sunshine Mrs Hardman had finalised on her plan of action for the disposal of Zadran's body and to that end called for the Base Commander to make ready the Chinook helicopter and it's two pilots for a late night departure on the hour's or so exercise.

Passing time until her nominated time of departure in the Chinook, Jessica Hardman and her MI6 group together with Damian, who was now able to walk albeit in great pain , took dinner with the Group Captain in his private quarters at which Damian related the details of his encounter with Zadran. Having heard the finer points it took a certain amount of restraint for 'B' not to be succumbed into accidentally divulging her secret knowledge of M.A.R.S. to the group.

(Read Jon Grainge's "Appointment in Cairo")

The night was dark. The hour was late : 2009 hrs. Time for Zadran's body to be escorted to the helicopter and the MI6 group to board, excluding Damian who felt the calling for a further period of rest, the short flight out to sea and back. As they slowly walked out across the concrete the Chinook pilots which included Flight Lieutenant Wright, having

seen their passengers leave the hanger, began their start-up checks in readiness to depart. Entering the rear doors the group found that Zadran's body had already been unceremoniously stowed aboard on the floor in an unmarked matt black plastic body bag.
Jessica took a few moments to stand back from the innocuous black package to quietly reflect on the inhuman incidents that the body before her had no doubt been involved in. It somehow gladded her confidence that the continual use of resources against terrorism was fully justified and worthwhile.
"Please strap yourself in ma'am we are about to taxy" the co-pilot informed Mrs Billgate-Hardman as he then asked for further information as to the intended flight plan for the Chinook.
"Of course" she replied.*" I want you to fly to the deepest waters within twenty five to thirty minutes flying time from here and then I will advise you"* she replied.
"Very well ma'am" and returned to the flight deck.
The engines wound up and engaged the rotors then after a short taxi the Chinook gently rose into the air and departed Akrotiri on a heading of one seven five degrees. Once levelled out at one thousand feet with confirmation that the helicopter had the dark waters of the Mediterranean passing underneath Jessica took to her feet to make an announcement to her group, still perplexed as to what they were doing and why ,*"Gentlemen, what is about to happen is unorthodox and will remain between the four of us and of the flight crew. Orders from the greatest height have been issued. The body of Zadran is never to be found so we are about to dump it into the deep sea. However before doing so I want you* (pointing to one of the thugs) *to put a bullet from the Egyptian pistol that Damian Arbuthnot gave you in*
Al-Arish into his gut. This is a precaution should in the very unlikely event of the body ever being discovered in

the future it will look like he was accidently killed by his own people in a firefight. We will also weight the body down with that lump of steel pipe over there which I had loaded into the aircraft earlier. Is all that understood?"
A rather muted mumble was heard in agreement before the thug asked,
"Why ma'am.? Why all this clandestine performance?"
"Ok you have the right to know I guess" she continued, *"Zadran is an extremely important figurehead to terrorist groups and can never be allowed to be found and used for martyristic proparganda or be ever relocated and used as a religious shrine. Now do you understand?"*
The gentle nod of his head conveyed his answer.
"Colonel will you do the honours please" Jessica requested arching her left hand in the direction of the body. Instantly he knew that he was to unzip the body bag and expose the abdomen region of the body. With that done Mrs Hardman made her way to the flight deck to advise the pilots that there would be a carefully placed gunshot and for them not to worry.

Bang! a single dull thud could be heard throughout the cabin as the thug discharged a single round from the Egyptian pistol into the exposed stomach. Very little blood ouzed from the wound. With that complete Colonel Hayward re-zipped up the bag.

Judging to be far enough out to sea and well away from possible prying eyes from the Cypriat island Mrs Hardman went back to the flight deck to order the opening of the rear doors. As the upper ramp door became fully opened this signalled the lower one to follow. It was the two thugs (MI6 interrogators remember) that dragged the body bag to the very edge of the lower ramp as simultaneously Mrs Hardman requested a small service of respect for those who had so tragically and innocently been murdered by the

jihadist that lay before them before the two thugs gently edged the body over the end of the ramp and into the void below. Very quickly the body disappeared into the darkness, gathering speed until it hit the dark waters of the Mediterranean with a tremendous splash. For the first few seconds the bag floated then bit by bit it started to submerge finally, with the Chinook now having embarked into the distant murk, sunk into the abyss to the bottom of the Mediterranean Sea one thousand metres below. A fitting lonesome end for a mass murderer.
Apart from the continual rotor thracking there was total silence aboard the half hour flight back to base. Not a word was spokcn in the reflective silence.
With her short mission now complete and the formalities with Akrotiri's base commander concluded, Mrs Hardman requested the 146 be readied for their immediate flight back to Northolt. The four and a half hour went without incident although the atmosphere on board during the flight was somewhat subdued.

With the dawn landing at Northolt complete the captain taxied the MI6 group to the waiting Jaguar on the far section of the airfield which in turn sped through the London rush hour traffic as best it could back to 'Babylon - on - Thames', this being the affectionate name for MI6 HQ on the Thames Embankment. Having safely dropped off
Lt. Col. Hayward and the thugs, Jessica ordered the car on to Downing Street where she would meet the PM for an impromptu early morning briefing before his appearance in the House for weekly questions.
With the Prime Minister, Denis Morrison satisfied with the outcome and final demise of the Jihadist Zadran,
Mrs Hardman further requisitioned the Jaguar for the journey down to Cheltenham for another impromtu meeting, but this time with her friend Florence D'Arcy. As she drove through Parliament Square Big Ben could clearly

be heard chiming ten times. The combination of the smoothness of the car and it's driver together with the activity of the last twelve or so hours sent the MI6 boss into a light slumber in the rear of the XJ denying her of the beautiful and tranquil countryside en-route to Gloucestershire.*"We are here Ma'am"* spoke the driver in a soft voice tinged with a sense of guilt in awakening his sleeping passenger of importance.*"Oh thankyou"* remarked Jessica as she opened her compact mirror for a final adjustment, *"Did you manage to radio ahead and confirm my arrival?"* she then asked.
"I did Ma'am and it is all arranged" he replied.

Both Florence D'Arcy and Jim Norris were in GCHQ's reception to greet 'B's' arrival and then escort her to Sir Philip's office on the top floor for the final briefing.
"Good morning Sir Philip. It with concluding news that I come to Cheltenham " she uttered as she greeted Philip Newman with a handshake and peck on his cheek.
"You have good news I hope. The Home Secretary has kept be abeam of some of the story but I am sure not all! but first coffee?" he advised.

The gathered soon settled into a general congenial conversation over the Kenko, however being brought to a head as Jessica raised her hands to quell the conversation,
"Enough of the niceties! Zadran he is dead" she abruptly addressed the group.
"Dead! how?" Florence asked.
"Killed in a firefight shootout in Egypt with the SAS" Jessica informed them, *"We buried him at sea where he could never be found. His colleague Asphan Rachid, the IT specialist we believe is dead also."*
Jim is his nieve wisdom then asked if there might now be a period of terrorist tranquility now that the head of

Al-Mawla has been cut off. Puffing out her rather large well formed chest and drawing breath, Jessica took this opportunity to inform the hierarchy of GCHQ that this was by no means the end, in fact it might just even be the beginning, of a new bout of activity.
"What do you mean Jessica?" asked Miss D'Arcy.
"You had all better sit down for this" advised 'B'.
" Sir Philip, Florence, you might just be aware that Mohammed X has taken over the Egyptian Brotherhood as President Kalesh has been imprisoned well ..... we have an British agent presently in Cairo liasing with Mohammed th..."
"*You don't mean Barton!!"* Florence interrupted.
"How the devil did you know!!" exclaimed Jessica with a look of surprise on her face.
"We picked up your agent's mobile transmissions Jessica!"
"You did well Florence, very well. Yes Barton, Group Captain Barton but this operation carries a triple A rating of secrecy. Even for GCHQ no further mention of this operation must ever leave this room. Both Mohammed and Barton are under continual surveillance and so sensitive is the operation that if ever uncovered the British Government will never admit to any connection or involvement with it. Can I have all your words on that?"
A general acceptance was forthcoming from all.
Then a final speech from 'B', the head of MI6,
"Sir Philip, this Zadran affair started with you at GCHQ and here now ends with GCHQ so on behalf of the safety of the British people please continue with your professional vigilence."

The End

Remember to read the completion
of this story in

"Appointment in Cairo"
available on:
www.blurb.com/user/store/hightrainman

APPOINTMENT in

CAIRO

"Revolution is in the Air"

(January 18th 2011)

Another action-adventure novel by

Jon Grainge

Author of

"Appointment in DOUZ"

"Appointment with the FAITH"

"Appointment in Puerto Banus"

2nd Edition

(2012)

The

"European Photo-Book"

collection

Jon Grainge

www.blurb.com/user/store/hightrainman

The

"European Photo-Book"

collection

Jon Grainge

www.blurb.com/user/store/hightrainman

Athens
GREECE
Crete
Nicosia
CYPRESS
Mediterranean
Sea
LEBANON
اللبنانيّة
السوريّة
SYRIA
Damascus
ISRAEL
מדינת ישראל
Jerusalem
أردن
Alexandria
Cairo
القاهرة
JORDAN
Sinai
Penin
Aqabah
Suez Canal
مصر
Nile
EGYPT
المدينة
Medina
Aswan Dam
Aswan
Euphrates

Overall map of the Middle-East.
(Note the locations of Damascus, Cairo and Tehran)

British Airways A380

American Boeing 777

Ravaged Damascus

Cairo

GCHQ

(Government Communications HeadQuarters)
Cheltenham

"The Doughnut"

Entrance Gate of GCHQ

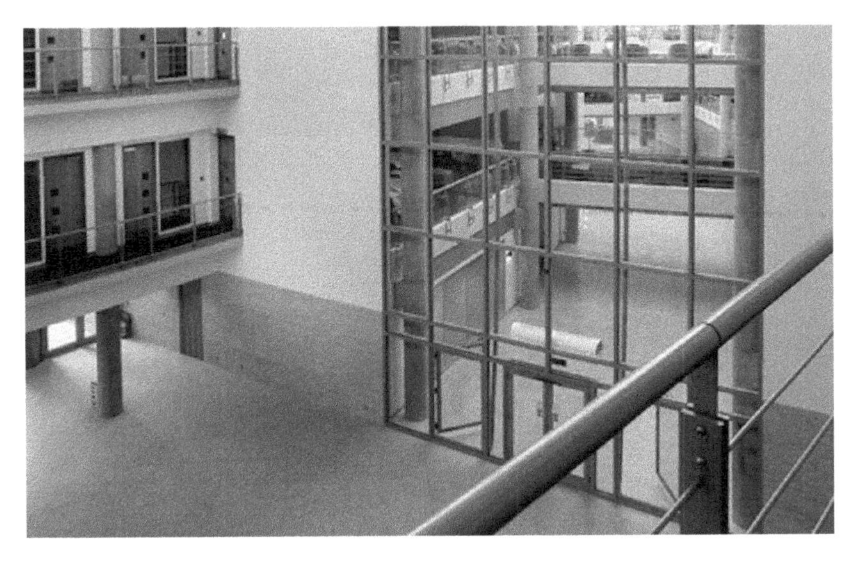

Interior of GCHQ

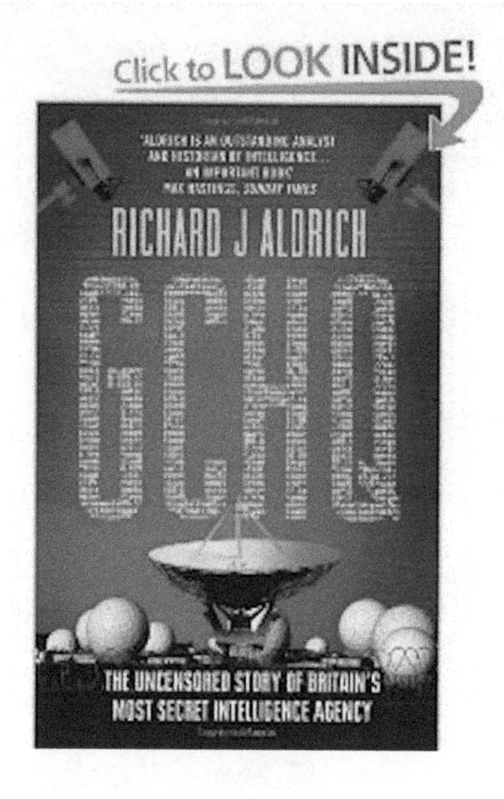
Click to LOOK INSIDE!
RICHARD J ALDRICH
GCHQ
THE UNCENSORED STORY OF BRITAIN'S
MOST SECRET INTELLIGENCE AGENCY

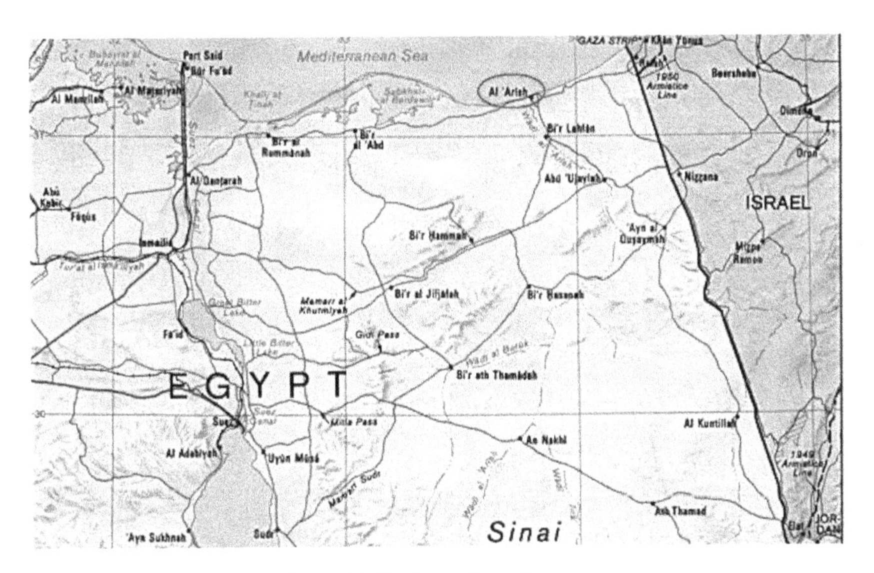

Al-Arish in Sinai

MI6 HQ
'Babylon-on-Thames'

Echoes from a Silent Enemy

The
"European Photo-Book"
collection

Action **NOVELS**

www.blurb.com/user/store/hightrainman

Appointment in DOUZ
"Death of a Colonel"

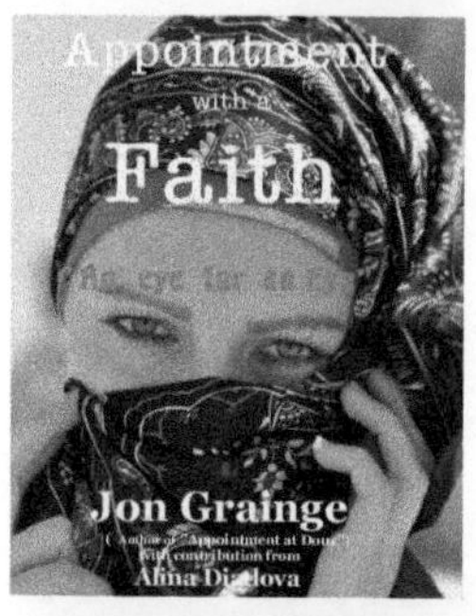

Appointment with the FAITH
"An Eye for an Eye"

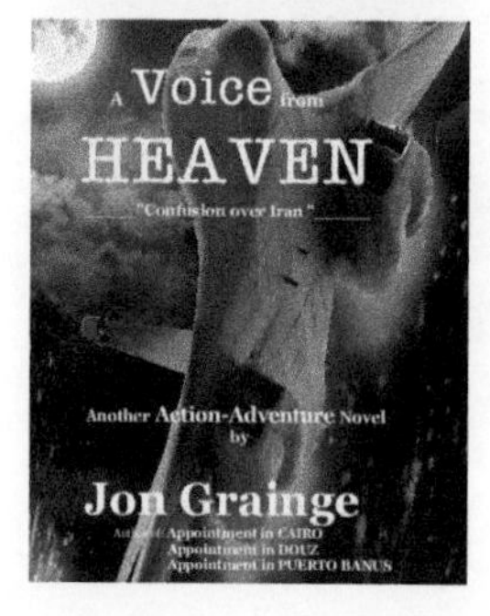

A Voice from HEAVEN
"Confusion over IRAN"

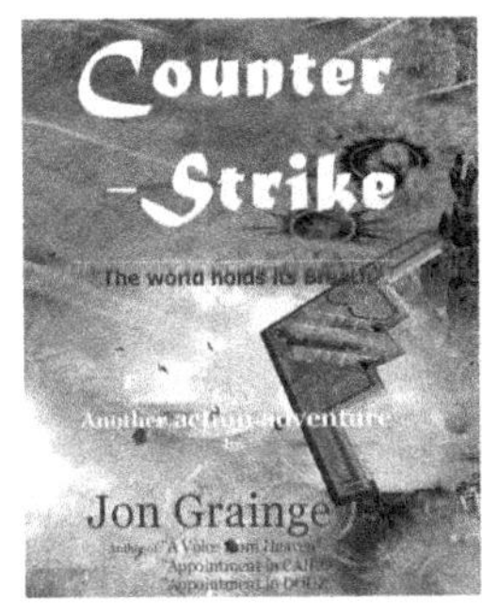

Counter-Strike
"The World hold's it's Breath"

Appointment in PUERTO BANUS
"Double Abduction"

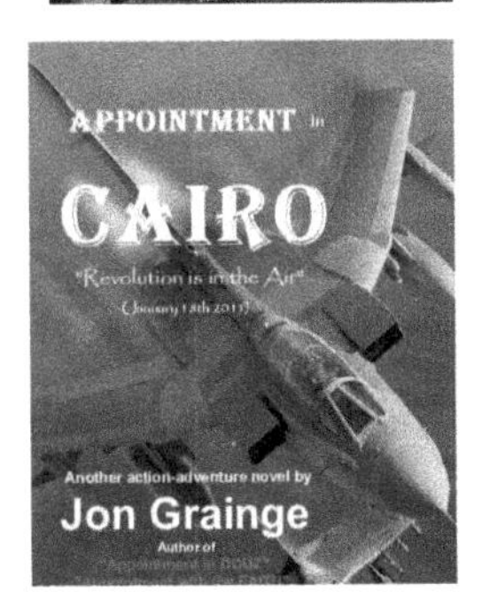

Appointment in CAIRO
"Revolution is in the Air"

About the Author

Born in the western suburbs of London Jon Grainge left school and entered the Royal Air Force where he enjoyed serving as a jet pilot for three years before furthering his rather varied career in European Marine sales,European Hotel marketing, and property sales in Marbella but has recently turned his hand to becoming a professional photographer and writer of Photo-Books under the title of The **"European Photo-Book"** collection

"**R.I.A.T.** 2013"

"**RAF** for the 21st century"

"**Men, Women** and their **War Machines**"

"**Air Tattoo** 2009-2012"

Feel free to investigate the

Photo-Books

of the collection

Lightning Source UK Ltd.
Milton Keynes UK
UKHW02n0217310718
326500UK00001B/18/P

9 781320 102179